BROTHER
with Benefits

MIA CLARK

Copyright © 2015 Mia Clark

All rights reserved.

ISBN: 1511771801
ISBN-13: 978-1511771801

Book design by Cerys du Lys
Cover design by Cerys du Lys
Cover Image © Depositphotos | avgustino

Cherrylily.com

DEDICATION

Thank you to Ethan and Cerys for helping me with
this book and everything involved in the process.
This is a dream come true and I wouldn't have been
able to do it without them. Thank you, thank you!

CONTENTS

ACKNOWLEDGMENTS

Thank you for taking a chance on my book!

I know that the stepbrother theme can be a difficult one to deal with for a lot of people for a variety of reasons, and so I took that into consideration when I was writing this. While this is a story about forbidden love, it's also a story about two people becoming friends, too. Sometimes you need someone to push you in your life, even when you think everything is fine. Sometimes you need someone to be there, even when you don't know how to ask them to stay with you.

This is that kind of story. It is about two people becoming friends, and then becoming lovers. The forbidden aspects add tension, but it's more than that, too. Sometimes opposites attract in the best way possible. I hope you enjoy my books!

STEPBROTHER WITH BENEFITS

1 - Ethan

IT'S TOO CUDDLY IN HERE. You know what happens when things get too cuddly? People start making out and having sex or falling asleep. There's something really fucked up about the contrast there, but that's what happens. I've seen it happen before.

In my case, I usually stop the cuddling from getting too cuddly and out of hand, but again in my case it usually ends up moving towards the making out or having sex end of the spectrum easily enough, too. Not right now. Nah. You want to know what's happening right now?

She's sleeping. That's it. We finished eating our pancakes and sausage, downed the orange juice fast, and kept watching Netflix. Now Ashley's curled up under the blankets, sleeping. I guess we aren't that close, all things considered. I'm still on top of the blankets, laying down next to her, watching what's going on.

I have no clue how someone can fall asleep while watching some biker gang do fucked up shit, but whatever. She's sick. I'll give her a pass. She deserves it.

Someone knocks on Ashley's bedroom door, then opens it before I can say or do anything. I glance up, trying to act all nonchalant, but the fact remains that I'm laying in bed with my stepsister. Kind of weird, don't you think? More weird when you remember we were arguing in front of our parents yesterday, and we've never really been all that close before now. I don't know. Whatever.

It's Ashley's mom. She sees me there, and sees Ashley sleeping, then lifts one brow, staring at us with peculiar interest. I can't say I blame her.

"Hey," I say. Be casual, don't fuck this up, Ethan. "What's up?"

"I was just coming to see if Ashley was awake," my stepmom says. "I know she slept in late yesterday, so I thought maybe she did today, too. I wasn't sure, though, what with everything that happened between her and Jake."

Oh yeah. That guy. Fuck him. What a stupid, undeserving prick. I should find out where he lives and kick his fucking teeth in.

"She's not feeling good," I say. "Sick or something? I don't know what. I made her some breakfast and we were watching TV, but then she fell asleep."

"Oh," her mom says. "Well, that's nice of you. Thank you, Ethan."

"Nah, don't--" I start to say more, but then Ashley fidgets in her sleep. Her arm stretches out and moves to my chest, wrapping around and hugging me. I stare at her hand. Well, what the fuck am I supposed to do now. "Don't uh... don't worry about it?"

Her mom laughs, but hides it behind her hand, trying to keep quiet. "Seems you make a good stuffed animal replacement," she says.

I roll my eyes, try to play it off. "Yeah, I'm cuddly as fuck. Who knew?"

"Ethan!" My stepmom glares at me for swearing, but she smiles to hide her laugh, too. "Do you want me to help? I can get one of her stuffed animals and we can do a quick switch if you'd like?"

I shrug. "Nah, I don't care. Whatever. She's tired, right? Sick, too. Should let her sleep."

"I was going to come find you after and see if you two wanted to go out to dinner with us tonight," Ashley's mom says. "Maybe tomorrow, though? That might be better. I thought we could

3

all do something together as a family. I know that might be strange for you. I hope you don't think I'm imposing on you and your father's life, Ethan. I never meant to."

Where's this coming from? I don't know. No clue. "Dinner sounds nice," I say. "Yeah, maybe tomorrow would be better. You're not imposing or anything. Sorry if I'm a jerk sometimes. I'm not used to this family thing yet."

"I know," she says. "And I know we've had this conversation before, but it's been a few years now and I'd like to say it again. If you feel weird with me being your stepmother, I hope we can at least be friends, too. I don't want to replace anyone important to you, Ethan. I don't want you to feel like you have to treat me a certain way or call me Mom if you'd rather not. I'm easy to work with. I'd like to be a part of your life, though."

"Yeah," I say. I don't know how to deal with this shit. What's with all these emotions and junk? Confusing as fuck, really. "I do like having you as a mom," I say. "I kind of like calling you Mom. If you don't mind, I'd like to keep doing it. I just... yeah... maybe we can play it by ear? Me and my dad have always been kind of like friends, I guess. Sort of. Except uh... yeah, you know."

"I know," she says. "I'm sorry you had to deal with that."

"It's cool," I say. It's not exactly cool, but it's been a few years now and I'm over it. "I thought things were going to get bad when I found out about you and him, but everything got a lot better. I really appreciate it. We're kind of screwed up here. I don't know how you and Ashley deal with us," I add, laughing.

"The most perfect things in life are created by our imperfections," my stepmom says. "You and your father are a part of that, too. Maybe you're both a little rough around the edges, but you're kind and unique and special in your own ways, too."

I roll my eyes. "Yeah yeah, thanks for the inspirational speech, Mom."

She giggles. "What I'm really worried about is you and Ashley. I know it's strange. I hope you two can get along? Maybe this is a good start?" she says, nodding towards the hand draped over my chest.

"She's alright," I say. "I wouldn't mind hanging out with her. I was going to ask her to come to the beach with me today, but then she was sick, so yeah, we're just chilling here. Sorry about the laying in her bed thing."

Her mom smiles. I don't know what she's smiling about, but it looks mischievous as fuck. What's up with that? She's got some devious machinations going on in her head or something. I don't like it. She's too smart, just like Ashley. Runs in the family, probably.

"You don't have to apologize to me," she says. "It's between you and her. You might have to apologize to her when she wakes up, but she looks comfortable right now while she's sleeping, doesn't she? I think it's fine. I know you've been through a lot, Ethan, but Ashley has, too. You both probably have more in common than you might think. Be careful with her, alright? I know we're not your real family, but I hope we can become close like one, and I hope you'll look out for her. My daughter is intelligent, but she's not always good at dealing with people or relationships. I think her breakup with Jake is hitting her hard."

"Yeah, he's just a stupid prick," I say. "I'm sorry, but I'm going to say it how it is."

Ashley's mom smirks. "Well, thank you. If I remember correctly, you're somewhat of a heart-breaker yourself, though."

"Yeah, I guess so. Maybe." Might as well admit it. "I know how it must look, but there's a differ-ence. I'm upfront with girls straight from the start. Maybe that doesn't make it better, but I kind of think it does. I really try not to hurt anyone, you know? I still do, so maybe it doesn't matter, but I try not to. I try to keep it simple."

"I think what probably hurts them the most is that they know they're missing out on an amazing experience with a wonderful guy," she says. "You might be upfront about everything, but that doesn't stop them from missing you when you leave, now does it?"

I'm not those things, though. I'm not amazing. I'm not wonderful. Girls don't miss me. Seriously, man, they're much better off without me. I'm an arrogant, cocky prick, a football jock asshole, and not a very nice guy. What more is there to say?

I don't want to start an argument, though. I shrug it off and grunt. Ashley's mom just smirks at me and gives me one of those looks. Yeah, you know the look? The ones moms give to their sons. It's family. She's my family now.

I can't ever tell her about what's going on with me and Ashley. I don't want to fuck that up. I don't want to ruin this, and I don't want her to hate me. Why'd I get myself into this situation in the first place? Because I'm stupid, obviously. No one's ever claimed I was smart.

"How about I go to the store and get some soup?" my stepmom says. "Biscuits, too. I'll make some up fresh for when Ashley wakes up, and I'll bring everything up for you both later. What do you think?"

"Sounds good," I say. "I bet she'll like that. Hey, if you don't mind, maybe grab some cheese, too? She likes melted cheese on her biscuits."

Her mom smiles wide and nods at me. "She does, doesn't she? I almost forgot. It's nice having you both back in the house. Your father and I missed you two."

"Yeah, it's nice being back," I say. I smile a little, too. Just a little. Don't get any wrong ideas here.

"Alright. I'll leave you two be. If you need me, you can call me or come downstairs. I'll tell your father to leave you two alone, so Ashley can get her rest."

"Alright."

"Thank you again for taking care of her," my stepmom says.

After that, she leaves. She almost keeps the door open slightly, but then at the last minute she turns around and closes it completely. It's cool. Whatever. I don't care.

I sneak my arm under Ashley's head and around her shoulders, pulling her closer to me. She sighs in her sleep and tugs at my chest a little more. It's fine. She's under the blankets and I'm on top of them. We've both got pajamas on. I swear this isn't as fucked up as it looks.

Nah, it's probably fucked up. I'm just taking care of my sister when she's sick, right? Stepsister.

Nah, that's probably even more fucked up. I don't know what's wrong with me.

2 - Ashley

I MUST HAVE FALLEN ASLEEP, but I'm awake now. I don't want to open my eyes, though. I want to go back to sleep. I want to dream nice dreams and forget everything else. It's easy right now, because Ethan is here with me. I thought it would be harder with him here, but it's not. It's easy because of how he's being when he's here, though.

He's not pressuring me. He's not staying too far away, either. He's actually very close. I have my arm around him and my cheek nestled against his chest. I'm not sure when that happened, but I like it. I should move away, I know it, but I don't, because I don't want to. I'm sleeping, right? I can blame it on that. If anyone sees us like this, I can just say I fell asleep. Maybe Ethan is asleep, too. It's an accident. No one can blame us for it, no one can judge us for this.

"Has she woken up yet?" my mom asks.

Oh my God, she's in my room? She can see me. I clench my eyes shut even harder and try to go back to sleep. If she knows I'm awake, I'll have to move away from him. I can't stay like this when I wake up.

"Nah, not yet," Ethan says. "I think she's waking up, though.

Why! Why did you say that, Ethan? I don't know why he said that. I guess I really do have to wake up now. I yawn and try to act normal. When I open my eyes and see myself laying on him, I scramble up and away like any normal stepsister in my situation would do. Right?

"What are you doing!" I say, sitting up and glaring at him. I try to sound properly indignant, but I'm pretty sure everything I just said sounds fake. Maybe I should have taken acting classes sometime. Life seems easier if you can pretend you're something else.

"Hey, look, you're the one who fell asleep on me," he says. "I was just trying to be nice."

"You?" I ask, rolling my eyes at him. "Nice? Since when has that ever happened."

"There's a first time for everything," Ethan says, smirking. "Don't get used to it, though. You're sick. That's the only reason."

Oh, right. I'm supposed to be sick. I kind of am sick. I still don't know how to deal with what I'm dealing with, but my head is a lot clearer now that I've taken a nap. I don't feel as stressed or hurt as I did before. I know I should, and I will soon enough, but right now I don't.

"What are you doing in here, Mom?" I ask, turning to her.

"I brought you soup," she says. "Some for you and some for Ethan. I thought it might help you feel better. Also, on Ethan's suggestion, I made some biscuits with melted cheese on top."

"Ooohh, I love those," I say. There's an entire plate full, too! They're really good, and I like them with soup since you can cut them in half and dip them in. The melted cheese just makes them better.

"Sounds like you're feeling a little better then?" my mom asks. "Are you hungry?"

I nod. "A little better. I'm hungry. How long was I sleeping?"

"Oh, a couple hours, I'd say. Right, Ethan?"

"Yeah, something like that," he says, shrugging.

"You should really thank Ethan for acting as your stuffed animal," my mom says, grinning. "He took it rather well, didn't he? I came in a few hours ago and you were like that, and then when I came back just now to bring up the soup, you were still there. You looked very comfortable."

Hours? What? And my mom knows? She saw all of it? She's playing it off, though. I think I know why. It makes more sense that way, right? It makes sense if it was an accident, and it makes sense if she doesn't think there's anything else going on be-tween us. Which is good, because I don't want her to know the rest. I don't want her to hate me or hate him or think we're gross and disgusting or wrong. I don't want her to keep us separated for what we've done. Yes, we're adults, but we're both living here for the summer, so we aren't exactly free to do whatever. Even if we were away and on our own, I don't think we would ever truly be free from societal taboos.

"Thank you," I say, mumbling to Ethan. "You didn't have to do that, though. You shouldn't have. I must have done it when I was sleeping. Sorry."

Ethan shrugs, then ruffles my hair like I'm a kitten or something. I bristle and act accordingly, pretending to hiss at him. He grins and I laugh. My mother smiles at us.

"Glad to see you two are getting along better," my mom says. "I was hoping you'd both see the light some day."

"No," I say. "Ethan's still a jerk."

"Yeah yeah," Ethan says. "Thanks for the reminder, Little Miss Perfect."

"Jerk."

"Princess."

I don't like how he says that. I don't like that I like how he says that. It's like a secret code shared between the two of us. He really shouldn't do that when my mom is here. I scoot further away from him for good measure, but my very own mother thwarts my plan of separation. She places a medium-sized tray table with two bowls of soup partway between the two of us, forcing us to come closer together so we can eat.

"I could only find the one," she says, apologetic. "I'm not sure what happened to the other one."

I know what happened to it. It's on my side of the bed on the floor, hidden from view. I could reach down and get it right now so that Ethan and I can have our own spots to eat, separate from one another, but I don't. Hopefully my mom doesn't see it.

"Which one is mine?" I ask.

While I'm staring at both bowls, my mom places the platter of biscuits between us, too. It's warm, but not too hot. I can feel the heat of it sinking into the blankets by my legs.

"I'll let you two decide," she says. "One is Italian wedding, and the other is beef and barley."

"Ooohh." This is difficult. "I like both. Um... what do you want, Ethan?"

He shrugs. "I don't care. I like both, too."

"You could share?" my mother asks.

It sounds so innocuous and polite, but my mind has other ideas. I've shared a lot of myself with Ethan over the past few days, haven't I? I don't think I'll ever be able to forget it.

"You both eat half, then you switch?" my mom adds. "I bought plenty more soup, so there's a lot downstairs if you're still hungry after, too."

I want to ask why we need to share and switch if there's plenty more soup, but I also kind of like the idea of sharing and switching, so...

"Share?" I ask Ethan, giving him a funny look.

"I'm keeping my spoon, though," Ethan says. "Who knows what kind of cooties you have?"

"Cooties! This isn't second grade, Ethan."

My mom laughs. "Shush, you two. Behave. I'm going back downstairs to help your father, but let me know if you need anything. You can call me or have Ethan come get me. I bought some medicine if you need any, too, Ashley. I hope you feel better soon."

"I feel a lot better now, Mom," I say. "Thank you. I'm sure I'll feel better by tomorrow."

I don't know if I will, but I have to. I have to because of what I'm going to do. I'm going to do it because of moments like this, too. I don't want to ruin them. I don't want to destroy them. I want to keep them precious and safe and mine, and to do that, I...

I reach for a biscuit and pull it apart, then dip some into my soup. I want to forget, at least for now. Ethan takes a biscuit and rips it apart, too, but then he dips it into... my soup.

"That's my soup," I tell him, scrunching up my nose.

"I thought we were sharing?" he says.

My mom is gone now. She closed the door behind her, too. It's just us.

"I'm sick, Ethan. Feed me?" I ask, smiling. I wonder if he'll do it?

"Are you serious?" he asks, giving me a funny look.

I nod quick. "Maybe?"

"Make up your mind, Princess!"

"I could be a little sick," I say.

Ethan picks up his spoon and dips it into my soup, then holds his hand beneath it while he brings it to my mouth. I open my lips and let him feed me like that. I swallow the soup and open my mouth again for more, but he gives me something else instead.

Leaning close, he kisses me quick. It's soft and fleeting, but nice and sweet, too. As soon as I start to kiss him back, he pulls away.

"What was that for?" I ask. "You're not supposed to do that."

"Nah, it's cool," he says. "Just kissing it better. That's how this works, right?"

"Again, this isn't second grade," I say, laughing at him.

"Yeah, you were a lot cuter in second grade," he says. "Too bad."

"I'm still cute!"

"Yeah, you're pretty cute," he says, shrugging. "Kind of sort of maybe a little."

"You don't think I'm cute?" I ask, frowning. It's kind of sort of maybe a little fake, but a frown is a frown.

"Nah, you're cute, Princess. Don't worry. Different kind of cute now, though."

"Can I have another kiss for being cute?" I ask him.

"Wow, greedy much?" he says, grinning. "Yeah, come here. Just one more."

He kisses me again, and I kiss him back. I wish we could stay like this forever.

"I'll need another kiss later," I say. "At least a goodnight kiss. That's all. It's not for any other reason."

"I'll give you a goodnight kiss alright," he says, growling at me.

"Ethan," I say, waving my spoon at him like a teacher's ruler. "You need to behave!"

"I'll get right to work on that," he says, rolling his eyes at me.

"These biscuits are really good, huh?"

"Yeah, the cheese is great."

"Thanks for telling my mom to add it," I say. "How does it taste with your soup?" I ask, but I'm already dipping my biscuit in his bowl before he can answer.

"Well why don't you just try it for yourself!" he says, grumbling as I taste and chew the biscuit dipped in his soup.

"It's good," I say. "Here, you try mine."

He does. I give him an extra spoonful of soup and feed him like he fed me before, too.

"Good, huh?"

"Yeah, it's good, Princess. Really good. You want to watch a movie or something?"

"Alright," I say. "You pick. Pick from your Netflix profile. I want to see what movies you like."

"You're saying you've never snooped on my profile?" he asks, grinning.

"Nope!" I say. It's a lie; I have.

"Liar."

"Nope!"

Mia Clark

3 - Ashley

ALL GOOD THINGS MUST COME TO AN END, and today is one of those things.

Ethan and I ate three bowls of soup. All different kinds, too. My mom bought a lot, apparently. Even though I'm not actually sick, the soup warms me and comforts me. I do feel better now, though I don't think it's going to last for much longer.

Ethan is asleep. It's late, and it's dark outside. Not too late, though. My mom should still be awake. I hope I can talk to her without Ethan's dad being around, though. I'm not sure if I can explain everything to both of them. It's easier if I only have to explain it to one person, and while I like Ethan's dad, I still don't feel as comfortable around him as I do around my mom.

I slip out of bed and sneak through the dark of night. I know these hallways by heart now, even if I've been away for awhile because of school. Before that I spent the better part of three years here. It was hard at first, but I grew to enjoy and appreciate it. It's easy to get used to a mansion when you used to live in a cramped apartment. Anyone could do it.

I tiptoe downstairs and towards the room with a light on: the living room. My mom is sitting in a chair in the room by herself. Further down the hall in another room entirely, I see another light on. It's Ethan's dad's office. He has to do work at home sometimes, and night is the easiest time for him to do it without missing out on spending too much time with my mother. I like that he cares about her like that.

My mom sees me coming into the living room and she smiles.

"Hey, honey, you feeling better?" she asks.

"Yeah," I say, smiling. "Thank you for the soup. It was really nice."

"I'm glad," she says. "Do you want some cough syrup? I bought some just in case, but you don't sound like you have a cough or a stuffy nose."

"Um... I think it was my chest?" I say. "I think maybe it was just anxiety, but I'm not sure."

"I understand," my mom says, smiling. "It happens to the best of us sometimes."

I wish she actually understood, but I know she can't. I can't explain everything that's happened to her. It's easier if I don't even try.

"Can I talk to you about something quick?" I ask her.

"Sure. Is something wrong?"

"No, um... not exactly, but sort of?"

She grins. "Uh oh. What's that mean?"

Uh oh is probably the appropriate response to this, even if she doesn't know it.

"Um... I sort of maybe promised a friend that I'd fly out to go see her?" I say. Her. That's it. It would sound stupid if I said I was going to visit a boy. I'm not visiting a friend, either, though, so maybe neither one matters. I've never lied to my mother before this, so whether it's one lie or two doesn't matter all that much; it's all equally bad.

"When?" she asks.

"I kind of maybe promised I'd go... tomorrow morning?" I say.

I don't have a lot of options. I'm being black-mailed into this. I thought I knew what kind of person Jake was, but apparently not.

I thought I knew what kind of person Ethan was, too. I definitely didn't.

This is difficult. I swallow hard, hoping my mother doesn't notice anything.

"That's going to be tough," she says. "I'd love to drive you, but we're waking up early tomorrow. Would it be alright if you had Ethan bring you?"

"Oh, no, um... I can just take a cab, Mom."

"Are you sure? I'm sure he wouldn't mind, Ashley."

"No, it's fine. I can take a cab."

"Alright," my mom says. "What about everything else? Are you sure you're feeling well enough to go? If you're sick, it might not be a good idea. Even small things can build into bigger ones if we aren't careful."

Don't I know it. That's how this all started in the first place.

"I won't be gone too long," I say. "I need to get a plane ticket, though. I know it's short notice but is that alright? I can do it right now."

"I think it'll be fine," my mom says, grinning. "I don't think your stepfather will have a problem with it."

"Alright," I say. "I'll go do that right now, then."

"Alright," my mom says. After a moment, she adds, "Is there anything else you needed to talk to me about, too? You know you can talk to me about anything, right?"

"Um..." I wish that were true; I don't think it is. "Actually..."

"Mhm?"

"Is it alright if Ethan sleeps in my room tonight?" I ask. "He already fell asleep. From earlier, I mean. I know that's kind of strange of me to ask. I can wake him up if you want, I just, um..."

"Is there something I should know?" my mom asks, lifting both her eyebrows. She stays like that for a second, but then she smiles. "I'm just teasing. Of course, that's fine. You're both adults. You can make your own decisions."

"I guess so," I say, muttering. "It's not like that."

It is like that, though.

"Not like what?" my mother asks. Is she being serious right now? I don't know.

"It's just sleeping," I say.

"Did I say it was anything besides sleeping?" my mother asks, coy.

"No, but I thought you'd be more upset?"

"If you thought I'd be upset, why'd you ask?" my mother counters.

Touche. I suppose she has a point.

"I just... I feel better when he's around, that's all. I know that he and I argued before, but he was actually really nice when you were gone. We..." I have to stop myself from blushing. "We went to go see a movie. At the drive-in. We got popcorn, too. And we went swimming in the pool. We ordered pizza and watched TV and went to a restaurant and had french fries and a steak and cheese sandwich."

"Just one sandwich?" my mom asks, grinning.

"We split it," I say. "He shared it with me."

"Ethan's a nice boy," my mother says. "I suppose he's a nice man now, isn't he? I know he has his rough spots, but I think we can forgive him that, don't you?"

"I think so," I say, smiling. "Just don't tell him I told you that."

"Oh, I won't," my mom says, pretending to zip her lips. "Your secret is safe with me."

"Good!" I say, giggling.

My mom yawns. "I'm getting tired. I think I'll head to bed soon. Do you need anything else first, Ashley? You should call to schedule a taxi for tonight as soon as you get your tickets."

"I will. Thanks, Mom. I should be all set. I don't think I need anything."

"Alright. Just let me know if you change your mind. You know where to find me."

"Alright," I say. "Um... can I have a hug goodnight?"

"Of course, honey. Come here."

I give my mom a tight hug and she holds me in her arms while we sway back and forth a little. It feels good. It reminds me of when I was younger. It reminds me of a lot of things.

"Goodnight," I say, whispering.

"Sleep well, Ashley," my mom says, hugging me one last time.

4 - Ethan

'M SLEEPING or dreaming or something. Again. Didn't we already deal with this before? What the fuck are you doing here?

Oh, wait. I'm awake now. I feel someone crawling into bed, which is kind of weird, but then I realize it's her. This isn't my bed, is it? I blink open my eyes and look around, and, yup, this is her room. It's her bed.

"Hey," I say. "Where'd you go?"

"I had to go to the bathroom," Ashley says.

"Didn't hear the toilet flush," I say.

"Um... I went downstairs. I needed to talk to my mom for a second, too."

"Alright," I say. "Yeah, I should get up and head to bed, too, then."

"No," she says. "Stay?"

"I know our rules and all of that, but do you think that's a good idea, Princess?" I ask.

"I asked my mom if you could," she says.

"Uh, what?" I can't even begin to comprehend that sentence.

"I told her you were sleeping and I asked her if you could sleep in here with me tonight. She said it was fine. She said we're both adults and can make our own decisions."

I laugh a little. It's not supposed to be funny, but it kind of is. "You think she really meant it?"

"No," Ashley says. "I don't know. I don't think she meant it in um... that... way..."

"Yeah, probably not. It's cool. Whatever."

She's under the blankets with me now. The lights are off. It's pitch black outside except for the faint twinkle of starlight. Even the moon is gone. We're completely alone together.

I know I should say I want to fuck her right now, and I wouldn't be opposed to that, but I kind of just want to lay down and cuddle with her and hold her in my arms and fall asleep. She's sick, anyways. Maybe tomorrow we can be a little more active, but right now I'm happy just spending the night with her in her bed. It's *her* bed and it's *her* special place. Why wouldn't I be happy to get invited to somewhere like that? Sounds pretty fucking amazing to me.

"Come here, Princess," I say, pulling her close.

She pulls up the blankets, covering us up to our chins. She wraps her arms around me, then stretches her leg out, pressing against my thighs, clinging close. I put my arms around her, too, and kiss the top of her head.

"Goodnight, Ethan," she says.

"Goodnight, Princess," I say.

A few seconds pass. Nearly a minute. Everything is quiet. My eyes are still open, though. I'm waiting for her to fall asleep before I go back to sleep. After awhile, she scoots closer to me and looks up.

"Kiss?" she asks.

I tip my head down so that I can kiss her, then I press my lips to hers. We lay like that, soft and silent, kissing. There's no urgency here, no immediate need, nothing crazy or lusty or any of that bullshit. That stuff complicates things. This is just a nice, soft kiss.

Our lips part, but she scoots up and kisses me again one final time before laying her head back on my chest.

"Goodnight," she says.

"Goodnight," I say, smiling.

Mia Clark

5 - Ashley

THE ALARM FOR MY PHONE goes off and I panic and scramble to turn it off before Ethan realizes what's happening. Thankfully I set the volume on low so that it would be quiet. It vibrates, too, but I don't think that will wake him on its own. I'm not even sure if I needed to set the alarm in the first place, because it's been nearly impossible for me to fall asleep. I kept closing my eyes and trying, but then I would open them, look at my bedside table clock, and less than twenty minutes passed. The night went on like this, over and over, until I did finally fall asleep, but...

I'm not asleep now. I'm awake and I need to leave. I have a plane to catch.

I leave my phone on the bedside table and sneak up and out of bed. Ethan sleeps softly, breathing even softer. He's laying on his back and my hand used to be across his chest, but I managed to free myself without him waking up. I slide my legs over the edge of the bed and slip away into the dark of night. Tiptoeing to my bedroom door, I grab my bag, open the door, and slip outside.

I want to take a shower before I leave, but I obviously can't do it in my room. I didn't think about this last night. Maybe I should have told Ethan he needed to sleep in his own room, but I'm not sure if that would have worked, either. It's fine, though. It's just a minor setback, but I have an idea. I tiptoe down the halls and head to Ethan's room, then sneak inside. Once I'm in, I close the door behind me and flip on the lightswitch.

I can use his bathroom. I can shower there. This is kind of where it all started, isn't it? It isn't exactly, but this is where I came when I agreed to our one week arrangement. I stripped down right over... here. I step there now, standing firmly on the exact spot. Placing my overnight bag on the floor by the foot of Ethan's bed, I decide this will be where I leave, too. This will be the beginning of my end. I pull off my pajamas and undress in the exact same spot as when I came to tell Ethan we could try his agreement. When I'm done, I pick my overnight bag back up and step into his bathroom.

I keep the light off in the bathroom, preferring the cool darkness instead. I leave the door open, though, so the light from his bedroom washes in, partly slicing through the darkness. Creeping in, I reach for the shower knobs, twist them, wait until the water is warm enough, and then I step in.

I don't have a lot of time, but I want to enjoy this while I can. I'm not sure what's going to happen to me after this morning. I don't know what Jake will want me to do. I need to figure out a plan, though.

First things first. If I agree to this, he needs to agree to some things for me, too. I want to see him erase the text messages I accidentally sent him, and I want to see him delete the recording of our phone conversation, too.

What if he made copies, though? What if he doesn't agree to delete anything and instead wants to continue blackmailing me? I think I should be able to steal his phone, even for a little bit, and delete everything myself, but I'm not sure what to do if he made copies. I'll have to figure that out as I go. That's my only option at the moment.

I wash off quick and rinse my hair. I shouldn't have rinsed my hair. Ethan doesn't have a hair dryer, and I don't want to risk going back into my room to get mine. I can't ask my mom to borrow hers, either. It's three in the morning, and she'd definitely wonder why I didn't just use my own.

I dry my hair as best I can given the circumstances, then tiptoe back into Ethan's bedroom.

I packed a few quick things in the dark before I snuck back into bed with him last night. Hopefully it's enough. I grab a pair of panties and a bra and slip those on quick, then a pair of jeans and a t-shirt. Nothing very fancy or nice. I don't want to wear anything nice for Jake. I used to want to, and sometimes I did, but not anymore. Maybe if I look unappealing enough, he'll give up this entire idea and let me leave.

I doubt it. I wish it were possible, but I doubt it.

I put my pajamas back in my overnight bag, turn off the light in Ethan's room, and slip away into the hall. Creeping to the stairs, then down, I sneak into the kitchen. I can hide here, I think. Sort of. I should eat something before I go, too.

There's a banana in the fruit bowl and a yogurt cup in the fridge, so I take those and grab a spoon quick, then go sit at the kitchenette table. I try to eat, and I do manage to take a few bites of banana and yogurt, but I'm not sure if I'm hungry anymore. I take one more bite of each, forcing myself, but afterwards I start to feel nauseous.

I'm really going to do this, aren't I? I'm going to sneak away, get on an early morning flight to a place I've never been, and let my ex-boyfriend blackmail me into becoming his sex toy for the next few days in order to keep the fact that I've been sleeping with my stepbrother a secret...

It sounds crazy. It really is crazy, isn't it? It is and it isn't. It's something that's actually happening, but I never thought anything like this would ever happen to me. It hurts to think about it. My heart hurts. My stomach hurts. I feel physically ill again. I start to gag a little, and then my mom walks into the kitchen, smiling.

"Really early flight, huh?" she asks.

I refrain from looking sick. I can't let her know. I can't have her trying to convince me to stay here instead.

"Yup," I tell her. "I thought it'd be the easiest."

"Did you sleep alright? It feels like we were talking in the living room just a few minutes ago."

"I slept alright," I say, lying. "I'm going to try and sleep on the plane, too."

"Is it a direct flight or do you have any lay-overs?" she asks.

"One stop," I say. "It's just for an hour. It won't be too bad."

"That's what everyone always says," my mom says with a wink. "Then there's delays for days." She grins and laughs. "I'm sure that won't happen. Ethan's father and I had a short delay on our flight back, but nothing too bad. Usually morning flights are a little better about delays. That's how it's always been for me."

For her. We never really flew much before she married Ethan's dad. After that, we all flew a lot more, though. In high school we used to take three or four vacations a year. I remember thinking it was crazy that we were allowed to miss school for a week like that, but I always made sure to get my homework assignments in advance so I could do it on vacation.

Ethan got his homework assignments in advance, too, but he never actually did them when we were gone. He'd always leave early, come back later for lunch, leave again, and be back for dinner.

Sometimes I thought about going with him. I was awake when he left, and I could have, but I stayed in our hotel suite instead. I stayed and I did my homework like I thought I was supposed to. I'm the good girl, right? I'm the girl who does her homework, gets good grades, and doesn't cause trouble. That's exactly who I am. That's always who I've been. It's not like I stayed in the hotel the entire time, but I always made sure to do my homework for the day first.

I think it would have been fun to go with Ethan, though. I never knew what he did when he left. I never asked and he never told me. He looked like he was enjoying himself, though. I don't know that for sure, but he always looked healthier and more vibrant to me, like an entirely different person than when we were trapped in a classroom.

And then when we came back home and went back to school he got yelled at for not doing an entire week's worth of homework, but that's another story entirely.

"Do you want the rest of this?" I ask my mother, holding up the remains of my banana and yogurt cup. "I'm not very hungry."

"No," she says. "Thank you, though. I just saw the light on in the kitchen and I figured it was you, so I thought I'd come say goodbye before you left."

"Thanks," I say, smiling. I do appreciate it, but it's hard to smile right now.

"Did you get everything you need? You're not forgetting anything, are you?"

I kick idly at the overnight bag by my feet. "I packed everything last night, so I should be fine."

"Alright. What time is the taxi showing up? I can drive you now if you want. I should have asked you what time the flight was last night. I didn't think you'd be leaving this early."

I glance at the clock on the microwave. "Oops, um... I should go wait outside. They should be here any minute."

"Might be easier that way," my mom says with a smirk. "The gates always catch people up. Especially this early. They might think it was a prank."

I laugh. "Maybe. Stranger things have happened."

"Give me a hug before you go, though," my mom says.

I stand up and go to her. It's so easy to hug her. I've always hugged my mother. I've always felt close to her, too. I've always told her everything about every part of my life. Even at college, I used to call her every single day to talk, and sometimes we'd talk for hours. My mom is like my best friend.

It would be easy to tell her everything right now. Easy to *say*, yes, but not easy to deal with it after the fact. I can't tell her. I don't want to. I don't want her thinking I'm a bad person. I don't want to lose my mother, and I can't lose my best friend. I need her so much, especially right now. I'm going to need her even more when I come back.

What about Ethan? What will he do? What's going to happen when I return? Is he going to hate me? Will he even ask me why I left, or will everything go back to normal once I'm gone? It's just like him, isn't it? It's just like those times where we were on vacation as a new family in high school and he left in the morning, then came back. I never asked him where he was going. I'm not sure if he'll ask me where I'm going.

That's what I want to believe, because it's easier, but I don't actually believe it. I'm not sure what I'm going to tell him if he asks, though.

A car honks outside. Oh no, it's the taxi! I hurry to grab my bag and my mom goes with me to the front door. She unlocks and opens it for me, leading the way for me to make my escape into the cool night air. I need to go now. I need to leave before Ethan realizes I'm leaving, because I'm not sure if he would let me. He would probably rather do something stupid and idiotic that would cause a lot of trouble. I kind of like that about him, but I don't know if that's the right way to deal with this. There's too much at risk right now.

"Have a safe trip," my mom says. "You're coming back soon, right?"

"Yeah, it's just a few days," I tell her. "I'll call you when I'm on my way home. Don't worry, Mom."

"Call me when you get there, too," she says. "I want to know that you got there safely."

"I'm sure I will!" I say, laughing a little. "Planes are pretty safe, you know?"

"I know," she says, grinning. "I'm your mother, though, and I worry about you."

"I know," I say. "Thank you."

The taxi honks again, louder and longer than before. Stop! I want to scream at him, but that would make this even worse. I heft my overnight bag up over my shoulder and run out and towards the front gate. I get there quick, then put in the code to open the little side door, and slip out and to the cab. A burly looking woman glares at me as I get into the car.

"Where to?" she asks. "Don't mean to be a bitch, but this is my last run for the night and I'd like to get home."

"Sorry," I mumble. "I just need to go to the airport."

"Sure, that works," she says. Before she pulls away, she taps a button on the meter to start the fare clock. "Should be close to twenty. You paying in cash or credit?"

I fish through my bag and pull out my cute little purse that I packed away in there. It's the only cute thing I brought, with everything else being plain. I grab my wallet from that and poke through. I should have enough.

"Cash is fine," I say, smiling.

"Sure thing, kid," she says, nodding.

The car pulls away, heading down the road to the highway, then to the airport. I'm gone.

6 - *Ashley*

W HAT DO YOU MEAN the flight's been delayed?"
I ask one of the attendants at my gate. "It
was just on time two seconds ago. They
started boarding the first passengers already."

She shrugs and apologizes and gives me one of
those sickly sweet smiles that all customer service
people seem to have. I've never minded it before,
but these are extenuating circumstances. It's not
that I want to hurry and get to Jake, but I want to
get there before he does anything drastic or foolish.
I want to make sure I'm there on time so that he
doesn't think I'm not going to show up, and then
send everything to my mom and stepdad.

And then if I do show up? If he's already done
it? I bet he wouldn't even tell me. He'd make me go
through with it anyways, lie to me, and when I
come back home...

My stomach lurches and I feel sick again. I grab on to the counter to hold myself up.

"Are you alright?" the woman asks. "You don't look so well. We have an emergency medical facility in the airport if you need it. I can just call someone and--"

"No!" I say, sharp and harsh and fast. "No. I'm sorry. Please. I just got a little off balance there. Why is the flight delayed, though? I know it's not your fault, but I'm kind of in a hurry. Can I switch to another flight that's leaving right now?" I ask.

"Inclement weather," she says, shrugging. I surely can't blame her for the weather, can I? That's the kind of look she gives me.

I glance outside through the large airport windows that run from ceiling to floor. It's sunny and bright, with barely a cloud in the sky.

"Um... what kind of inclement weather is that?" I ask, purposely glancing over her shoulder.

She looks, too. When she turns back, her face is slightly pale and she swallows hard. "It's um... What was it again, Bobby?" she asks the man next to her.

"Inclement weather," he says. "Miss, I realize it looks nice out, but the dry air can sometimes cause issues with mechanical functions. The rubber sockets and widgets can dry out. It's become incredibly dry out all of a sudden, so we just want to check to make sure everything is in working order before takeoff. I hope you understand."

"We can see about switching your flight," the woman says. She scans through a quick list on her computer. "It'll take less time just to wait, though. The next flight going to your destination isn't for an hour and a half."

"I guess I'll wait," I say, scrunching up my brow. "Do I have time to get a magazine, though?"

The female attendant smiles. "Sure. As long as you're quick. We'll begin boarding again shortly. I'd recommend going to the gift shop right across the way just to be safe."

It's right behind me. That's where the gift shop is. I was in it before this, but then I heard them boarding, so I hurried out, and...

I go back, clutching my overnight bag tight in my hands. It's all I have left. It's the only part of me I have here. Everything in it is currently everything I own. All the rest of my things back at home seem so far away and lost right now.

I head to the magazine rack to check what they have. I don't actually want to buy a magazine, though. I just want to get away and lose myself for a moment. I want to pretend my life is regular and not really screwed up. It is, though. This is screwed up.

I grab a magazine. I'm not sure what it is. I don't care. Heading to the checkout counter, I put it down. The man at the register starts to ring me up.

"Anything else?" he asks.

I glance at a rack of personalized keychains next to the register. I don't know why I look. I shouldn't have looked. I grab the one that caught my eye and hand it to him.

"For someone special?" he asks with a grin. "It's always fun to get gifts for people when you travel. I bet he'll like it. Do you want a bag for these?"

"Yes, please," I say. I hand him the money.

He puts my magazine in the bag first, but hands me the keychain instead. "Might want to put that one in your pocket so you don't lose it."

That's true. I don't want to lose it. I put the keychain in my pocket, take my change from the man, and take my bag with my magazine, then head back to the airplane gate.

I can feel the press of the keychain against my skin through my jeans. It feels tight against me, almost as if he could leave an imprint on my skin with it.

The keychain says "Ethan" on it. It has a picture of the city skyline at night, with lights in all the buildings. I don't know if I'm going to give it to him when I come back, or if I need it for myself to remember him while I'm gone.

I need something. I want to feel him against me, again. I want to feel the press of his lips against my skin. I want to feel him inside me, feel him close to me, feel him next to me, feel him holding me.

I can't, though. This keychain is the best I can do.

7 - *Ashley*

I'M HERE. FINALLY.

This is good. Maybe.

I take my bag and head to the baggage claim area. That's where Jake said he would meet me when I sent him a text about my flight late last night. I hurry there, even though I don't have any baggage to claim. My overnight bag is with me, slung over my shoulder. It's not much, but it's enough.

I open it a little and search through it for my purse, then look through that for my phone, but it's not there. Maybe it fell out. I need to call my mom, though. I can't right now. There's too many people around me and I can't just stop or they'll run me over. I hurry with the surge of the crowd while zipping my bag up, heading to the baggage claim area.

I see him when I get there. It seems like a long walk, but it also seems like I'm there in an instant. Jake sees me, too. He smirks as I approach. I stop just short of standing directly in front of him. There's still a good amount of distance between us. I hope it'll stay like that. It doesn't. He closes the gap and comes up right next to me.

"Glad you showed up," he says. "I thought you might have bailed. I didn't want to have to do anything drastic."

"You won't tell anyone, right?" I ask. "Jake, promise me you won't. If you ever cared for me at all, then you won't."

He gives me a weird look. "What's with the melodrama?" he asks. "This is about sex, plain and simple. That's what it's always been about, but you were too prude before. If this is the only way I can get what I've wanted for a long time, then that's it. Don't try to make it into something it's not."

"We did have sex, though," I say. "We did a couple of times."

"Yeah, and you cockblocked me more than a dozen times, Ashley. Not to mention you always made excuses, like having to do homework or go help out your professors. I wouldn't even really call what we did dating. We went on a few dates that were barely dates, and you gave it up twice, then I dumped you."

"Are you always this much of a dick?" I ask him. Maybe that's bold of me, but I don't care anymore. "I used to think you were nice. I don't know how."

"I do," he says. "Because you don't know any better. You're smart, I'll give you that. You've got no common sense, though. You can't even see when someone's just being nice to you to try and get what they want. You're intelligent, but you're an idiot, Ashley. I bet that's how your precious little Ethan took advantage of you, too. That's really messed up, Ashley. I can't believe you did that."

"He... he did not!" I say. I try to slap him, but he grabs my hand and stops me. "He did not. Ethan didn't take advantage of me. He's not like that."

Jake squeezes my wrist hard. It hurts. He pulls it down and drags me away to somewhere quieter. I stumble and scramble to keep up. I want to scream at him, but he's right. I can't cause a scene. He's still got leverage over me. I hate him, but I need to figure out how to stop him first. I need to find a way to stop this, and...

We're in a quiet, secluded corner. I don't think anyone can see us here. Jake throws my wrist down, then sneers at me.

"You really are that stupid, aren't you? I thought maybe I was just that good at manipulating you, but you really *are* that stupid," he says. "Huh."

I start to say something, but he claps his hand over my mouth and stops me. Then he pushes me against the wall. His body presses close to mine and his other hand grabs at my breast, squeezing it through my t-shirt.

"You had to wear the ugliest thing you could find, didn't you?" he asks. "You think that'll stop me? I've seen you naked before, Ashley. You're going to be naked again soon, too. You're going to be naked on my bed and I'm going to fuck you as much as I want for the next two days. If it makes you feel better, you can even call me brother while we're screwing. How's that sound? Good?"

I shake my head and squeeze my eyes shut. I try to speak, but his hand is on my mouth still.

He smirks, wicked, and pulls his hand away to let me talk. "You have something to say?" he asks.

"You can't do this," I say. "You can't do this to me."

"I can't? Why not?" he asks, mocking me. "You're the one who came here, Ashley. I'll stick to my part of our bargain, but you're the one who came here. We had a deal. Who exactly do you think is going to stop me?"

I don't know. No one. Anyone. Me? I can't, though. Jake is stronger than me. I might be able to overpower him for a second, but then what? If I make a scene in the airport, he'll just pull his phone from his pocket and two seconds later he'll have sent the text messages to my mom and stepdad. And then what? I'll be stuck here, trapped and alone, with nowhere to go. I can go home, but will I even have a home to go back to? Will everyone hate me? Will my mom hate me and will Ethan hate me and...

"Yeah, who the fuck is going to stop this prick? Oh, shit, I guess that would be me, asshole."

Um... huh?

Jake lets go of me. Sort of. He doesn't let go of me so much as someone pulls him away from me. I blink and look up just in time to see a powerful fist collide with Jake's jaw. My ex-boyfriend crumples to the ground immediately, falling flat. He twitches and lays there for a second, but then finds himself and starts to sit up. He looks groggy and almost drunk, but he manages to sit.

It's Ethan. Ethan is here? Ethan punched him. What's Ethan doing here? How is he here?

Ethan grabs Jake by the front of his shirt and pulls him up, staring down hard at him.

"You fuck with her again, I'll kill you," Ethan says. "Understand, loser?"

Jake tries to talk, but it's like his jaw doesn't work. He manages to open his mouth after three tries.

"Who the hell are you?" Jake says, his words slurred.

"You don't need to know who I am," Ethan says. "You even so much as look at my sister the wrong way again, and I'll send you to the ICU. Nah, scratch that. If you even look at her number in your phone the wrong way, I'll know, I'll come find you, and I'll kick your fucking ass. Got it?"

"Fuck--" Jake starts to say. Ethan throws him to the ground and tosses him away, though. Jake breathes out the last word before the air is knocked from his lungs. "--you..."

Then Ethan grabs me. He takes my elbow in his hand and pulls me away from the isolated corner we're standing in, then drags me back to the crowded parts of the airport.

"Holy fuck, what the hell were you thinking?"

8 - Ethan

(hours before)

Holy FUCKING FUCK fuckity fuck stick hell on a shit basket. Why does no one want me to sleep?

First it was some stupid fuck honking his horn outside. Fucking drunk. He did it twice, too! I barely heard it the first time, but then I was drifting my way back to sleep when he did it again. Louder, too, the stupid prick.

That's not the worst of it, though. I fell asleep after that. You know that feeling when you fall asleep, but then you wake up suddenly from some-thing *right* after? Like, you literally just fell asleep, and then something wakes you up. Yeah, this is that. That's what happened.

What the fuck is that noise? It's annoying and buzzing and quiet but not quiet enough. Something rattles around on... something else. I don't fucking know.

Oh, it's a phone. It's not my phone. I'm not even in my room.

"Holy fuck, Princess, shut your damn phone off. I'm trying to sleep."

It's then that I realize she's not even here. I'd know if she was here. I'd feel her sleeping on me, first off. I've slept alone enough times to know what sleeping alone feels like, and right now I'm sleeping alone, which is kind of fucked up because I shouldn't be.

I open my eyes and look around and see the phone vibrating and buzzing. It's obviously an alarm. I don't know why she set an alarm for this early. The time on the clock on her bedside table says it's a quarter before four in the morning.

I fling myself over to her side of the bed, grab the phone, and click to shut it off. That's all well and good, but where the fuck is she, too? I have half a mind to get up and find her ass and drag her back to bed. Yeah, that's what I'm going to do.

I check the bathroom first. Nope, not there. Why's this have to be so difficult? I get up and stumble into the hall and go to my room. Nah, not there, either. I check the bathroom and someone's been using my shower, though. What the fuck is up with that? No clue. I'm going to get to the bottom of this, though.

I go to the stairs and look down. There's a light on in the kitchen. She's hungry? Midnight snack or something? Sure, I can buy that. I head downstairs, go into the kitchen, and...

Nah. It's Ashley's mom. My stepmom. She smiles at me.

"Hey, Ethan. You're up early. Something wrong?"

"Uh... maybe?" I say. "You seen Ashley?"

"She just left," her mom says. "She said she's going to visit a friend for a few days. She didn't tell you?"

"What? A friend? *What* friend?" I feel like I should know if Ashley was going to visit a friend. I guess she doesn't have to tell me everything, but it's kind of fucked up that she didn't tell me this one thing.

Her mom shrugs. "I don't know. She came to me last night and asked if it was alright. I sort of got the feeling it was a last minute thing, so maybe that's it. She bought the plane tickets last night and left just a little while ago."

"Whoa, hold up, a plane? Where's this friend of hers live?" This is really suspicious. I don't mean to be a jerk about it, but I know she doesn't have that many friends. I'm sure she could have made some in college, and that's cool, but I'm pretty sure she would have told me she was going to visit one of them, too.

Her mom shrugs. "I'm not saying you should, but if you want to be nosy, you could always check the computer browser history."

"You're telling me to snoop on Ashley's private business?" I ask. Don't know why I'm asking this, because I was going to do it anyways.

"I'm not *telling* you to," her mom says, coy.

"Alright," I say. "I will."

Her mom follows me. Apparently I've got an accomplice in this invasion of privacy. Whatever. We check. Where the what the fuck?

"Where's this?" I ask. "Something important there?"

"Oh," her mother says, confused. "I don't know if this is it, but that's where Jake lives. Right by there. Ashley told me once when they first started dating. That's strange."

"Strange as fuck," I say, gritting my teeth, glaring at the computer monitor.

"Maybe they made up?" her mom says. "Also, please don't swear like that, Ethan."

"Yeah, uh... no," I say. "Sorry for swearing. They didn't make up, though. I'm sure of it."

Her mom shrugs. "I don't know. I'll ask her when she calls, though. I'll keep an eye out for a call around the time it says she's going to land. So... just a few hours. That's not so bad. We can get to the bottom of this, Ethan."

When she calls? But Ashley left her phone upstairs. Which, I realize, was an accident. I'm about to get a whole lot snoopier here. Charlie Brown's dog has nothing on me.

"Excuse me, but I've got to go do something quick," I say.

"You do?" her mom asks, laughing. "Ethan, it's almost four in the morning. I hope what you're going to do is go back to bed. I'm sure everything is fine."

I grunt. I've found that whenever you don't know what to say, it's easier to just grunt. Women take it as some sound of reassurance, I guess? I don't know. Easier to grunt than explain every little thing, though. Especially now since I can't exactly explain anything to her.

I bound up the stairs, two at a time, then jog to Ashley's room, hop on her bed, grab her phone, and start playing private detective. This isn't hard. The password for her phone is stupid. She knows I know it. I don't know why she never changed it. I'm glad she didn't change it.

I scroll through shit, check a bunch of junk, go to text messages. Yeah, there's some from Jake. Also some to Jake. Holy fuck, is that her? What the hell is she doing sending him naked pics for? When the fuck was this? I check the timestamp and it was yesterday. Technically the day before yesterday now. This four in the morning shit is really fucking me up.

Mia Clark

Ethan, I can't wait to give you a blowjob later. Maybe I'll come into the shower right now and give you one. How naughty would that be? Giving my brother a blowjob in the shower while our parents are sleeping right downstairs? Would you like that? Text me back when you get this and tell me what you want to do to me, too.

Alright, that's to me. Yeah, I can't fucking wait to feel your lips around my cock either, Princess. I grin at the thought. It's a real good thought.

She mentions me in this text, but she sent it to Jake? I think I'm getting a better picture here. Reading through a few more texts makes it all crystal clear.

Wow. What a prick. He thinks he can do that to her? Nah, she's mine. I don't give a fuck what that means. I don't even know what it means. He's not going to fuck with her like that, though.

Yeah, she's just my stepsister. We're not blood-related. We don't have a bond like that. I don't care. She's still my sister. She's like family. Maybe she is family. Yeah, that sounds fucked up. Sorry? She's more than that, though. She's my beautiful fucking Princess and if he even so much as touches her I'll break every single one of the dirty asshole's fingers. He's done. He's a dead man. I will not stand for this.

No one can fuck with Ashley without paying the consequences. He's in for a world of pain. I just

54

need to figure out how to do this. It shouldn't be too difficult. I remember what flight she took and what airline she was on, so it should be pretty simple, actually.

Mia Clark

9 - *Ashley*

(after, in the airport)

W HAT ARE YOU EVEN DOING HERE, Ethan?" I ask. He's dragging me through the airport and bringing me to one of the ticket counters.

"Rescuing your ass, Princess," he says.

"I didn't ask you to rescue me!" I shout at him. I didn't think I was being that loud, but people start to look at us. Hushed, I say it again, "I didn't ask you to rescue me, Ethan. You don't understand what's going on."

"I understand," he says. "Just shut the fuck up for a second, alright? Sorry to be an asshole about it, but we're leaving. I'll explain everything to you after."

"You *are* an asshole," I say. "Thank you for saving me, though."

He grins, cocky and arrogant and just like himself. I laugh and roll my eyes at him. I feel better already. I feel lighter and lifted, completely unlike the dread and anxiety I felt when I stepped out of the airplane.

We wait in line. Ethan looks like he's going to start strangling people and shoving them out of the way, but thankfully the line isn't that long. We get to the front soon enough. The woman behind the counter balks when Ethan glares at her. I don't think he's glaring at her so much as he's just been glaring this entire time at nothing in particular. Unfortunately she's in front of him right now, though.

"Sorry," I say to her. "He's a little on edge at the moment."

"Fuck off," Ethan says.

I stick my tongue out at him. He rolls his eyes at me in return. And then he kisses me. It's fast and quick, but passionate and intense, too. The woman at the ticket counter gapes at us, then she starts to giggle.

He... he kissed me? Oh my God, Ethan kissed me, and right here in front of everyone. Oh my God. No one knows, though. They don't know he's my stepbrother. It's fine. It's...

"Tickets," Ethan says. "We need two plane tickets." He tells her where. She browses through a list on her computer.

"When do you need them for?" she asks.

"Right the fuck now," Ethan says. He doesn't say it angrily or annoyed, just very calm and matter-of-fact. It sounds so strange, almost offensively inoffensive. It's weird.

"Um... we... we have something for thirty minutes from now?" she offers. "That should be enough time for you to get through security if you're fast. Do you have any bags to check?"

"You want to check your bag, Princess?" Ethan asks, turning to me.

"No," I say, shaking my head.

"Oh, sorry," the woman says. "This happens sometimes with flights that are about to leave. There's only one seat left, though. The other was just booked."

"No," Ethan says, firm. "There's two."

"No, really. I'm sorry, but there's just one. I can get one of you on this one and another on the next one in... three hours? Is that fine?"

"Ethan," I say to him. "I don't mind waiting. Really."

It doesn't matter if we wait. No matter what, it's going to be terrifying once we get back. Maybe it's better if we wait.

"Can everyone just hold on a second?" Ethan asks. "Please. I've got to make a phone call."

"Um, sure?" the ticket woman says.

Ethan reaches into his pocket, grabs his phone, and dials a number.

"Yeah," he says to someone on the other end. "Yeah. Uh huh. She says there's only one. I need you to talk to her. Get this sorted out. Right? Yeah."

"Um...?" the ticket woman stares blankly at Ethan.

"Hey," Ethan says to her. "Your boss wants to talk to you. Here." He hands her the phone.

"My boss?" she asks. She holds the phone up to her ear. "Hello?"

Her eyes widen. "Oh my God, Mr. Wentsworth. Yes, sir. I didn't know, sir. Sorry, sir."

"Mr. Wentsworth?" I ask Ethan.

"Yeah, he owns this shit," he says. "Him and my dad are friends. They do business a lot."

"He owns... what?"

Ethan shrugs. "You know? The planes. The airline. Everything."

"Ethan! You seriously called up the *owner* of the airline to get her to give us tickets? Don't you think that's a bit much?"

"Nah, not really."

Something dawns on me. "Inclement weather? That was you, wasn't it? I knew it sounded stupid. It was beautiful out. What sort of inclement weather is that? There's not even such a thing as a rubber widget on an airplane, I bet."

"Is that what they said? Listen, Princess, I needed your flight delayed. Had to catch up, you know? I got a direct flight here, but even still it landed five minutes after you. You have no idea how fucking pissed I was about that. They said they couldn't fly the plane any faster, though. I would have taken my dad's company jet, but they need time to prepare and shit. Wouldn't have worked."

"You're unbelievable," I tell him. "I really can't believe you did all of that. Are you crazy or something?"

"Yeah probably," Ethan says, grinning. "You want to make something of it, Princess? I'll argue. We can argue right now. All the way to the departure gate, then all the way back home on the plane, and then I'll sit your ass in a taxi and argue with you all the way back to the house. I don't give a fuck. There's consequences to arguing with me, though. You'll like them, don't worry. You might be screaming something, but you won't be mad at me anymore."

Is he... oh my God, yes he is. Sex! Is that all he thinks about? I blush and then I slap him on the cheek. It's not very hard. He grabs my hand and pulls it to his lips, then kisses my fingertips.

"Yeah, I'll show you rough later, Princess," he says. "Keep it up. Keep that anger inside you. I want to put it to good use."

"Shut up," I say, turning away from him. "Don't say stuff like that."

He takes my chin in his hand and makes me look at him. I think he's going to say something, but he doesn't. He kisses me instead. I... what? This is the second time! I don't even think he realizes what he's doing. Ethan is crazy. He's gone insane. He really really has.

"Yes, um... Mr. Colton?" the ticket woman says, interrupting us.

"Hold on," Ethan says. To her, not me. To me, he goes back and keeps kissing me.

"Ethan!" I hiss between my teeth through our kiss.

"Fuck, you're difficult. Can't you just enjoy a good thing?" he asks.

"Buy the damn plane tickets! Cut it out!"

"Whoa, feisty! Didn't think you had it in you."

I glare at him. He grins at me. Ugggghhhh!

"Yes, um... Mr. Colton, I apologize about before. We've just arranged for one of the other passengers to take a later flight, so we have two seats left. The plane will wait for you to board, too. You don't have to worry about missing it, but please try to be prompt."

"Look, we're not going to fuck around here," he says. "As soon as you give me those tickets, we're going."

"Um, right. Alright. I just need to see both of your IDs and a credit card or cash if you'd prefer."

Ethan reaches into his pocket and gets his ID to hand to her. I give her mine, too. He pays with a credit card.

"How about a first class upgrade?" he asks. "That available?"

"No," she says. "Um... I'm very sorry, because I did try at first." The look in her eyes says something like, 'Please don't call Mr. Wentsworth again.'

I nudge Ethan with my elbow and whisper in his ear. "Be nice to her, please. She's trying her best."

"I am being fucking nice," Ethan says. He even asks her! He asks her! Who does that? "I'm being nice, right?"

She smiles and nods but doesn't say anything.

"It's alright," I tell her. "He's not being nice. He knows it, too. He's just a rude, arrogant asshole. Don't worry. I know you can't tell him that, because this is your job, but I'll make sure to tell him it for you. A lot of times. As many times as I can."

The woman looked scared before, but after that, she giggles.

"Oh, funny jokes, huh?" Ethan says. To the ticket woman, he adds, "Hey, sorry about that before. I didn't mean to be a dick. You *are* doing a great job. I really appreciate it. If you ever need a favor or something, here's my number. My family knows people. I've got you covered."

He takes a card out of his pocket. It's one of his dad's business cards. Ethan grabs a pen from the ticket counter and writes his cellphone number on the back, then hands it to her.

"Um... thank you, Mr. Colton," she says.

"Don't you dare think about calling to try and seduce him, though," I add. "No flirting or anything like that."

"Of course, um... Mrs. Colton?" she asks. "Are you his girlfriend? I'm sorry, I didn't think to ask." She checks my ID quick, since she still has it. "Oh, Mrs. Banks."

"Yeah, girlfriend," Ethan says. "We just started dating, but we've known each other since second grade. Cute, huh? Real romantic."

"Awww!" she says. "That is nice. I've known my fiance for a long time, too. We met in middle school, but we didn't start dating until we ended up going to the same college together."

"Is he a nice guy?" Ethan asks. "I can rough him up for you if he needs. I don't mind. I owe you one, right?"

She laughs and winks. "No, he's nice. I'll tell him he better stay on his best behavior, though."

"Yeah," Ethan says, smiling. "Sounds good."

We get our tickets. Everything is good now. Sort of good. It's good *for* now, but I don't know how long now is. Now is at least as long as it takes for us to fly home and take a taxi back to the mansion.

We go through security and head to the boarding gate. We're the only ones there, but they're waiting for us.

10 - Ethan

LMOST AS SOON AS WE GET ON THE PLANE, I realize there's a serious problem. I lead the charge here, heading to my seat, with Ashley walking quietly behind me. I check my boarding pass again and head to the right place, and...

What the fuck is up with this? There's only one empty seat here. Two seats total on this side, one is empty, and it's definitely mine, so uh... yeah?

I turn to Ashley. "Hey, what seat number are you?"

She checks her ticket quickly. "Um, K4," she says.

Do you know where K4 is? It's a lot farther along than this. We're at F2 right now, and K4 seems like forever away. I'm none too pleased about that, but I suppose there's not much I can do, now is there? I seriously have to spend the entire flight home sitting by myself over here with Ashley way in the back? Yeah, I guess so.

"It's fine," she says. "It's really not a big deal, Ethan."

"Yeah, I guess so," I say.

At least I have an aisle seat. That's nice, right? No, not really. I sit down and introduce myself to the man next to me while Ashley heads further down to her seat.

I watch her go, more than a little pissed off. I came all this way, did all of this, and for what? It's not like I need to be next to her, but I really want to sit next to her right now. I'm sure the guy next to me is cool and all, but he's not Ashley, and I doubt he's going to want to cuddle or anything. That's sort of a drawback. He's not much of a looker, either. Ashley's way cuter.

Ashley brings her bag with her, putting it under her seat. She's got a window seat, and there's a little old lady next to her. At least it's not some young guy. Definitely no flirting is going to go on, unless that old woman is a freak, which I guess is possible.

But still... man...

"Hey," I say to the guy next to me. "I'll be right back. Maybe."

He shrugs. That's what I would do, too. Shrug. He doesn't know me. It doesn't make any difference to him what I do, as long as the plane gets to where we're going safe and sound.

I march down the aisle to Ashley's seat. She's looking out the window at first, but when I clear my throat she turns my way.

"Ethan?" she asks.

I'm not talking to her right now, though. Not yet. Soon. Hold on, Princess, I'll get to you in a second.

"Excuse me, ma'am," I say to the little old lady. "Would you mind switching seats with me? Mine's right up there." I point to it.

The woman smiles at me and glances over at Ashley. "Oh, is this your girlfriend?" she asks.

"Yeah," I say. "That's her."

Ashley mumbles and blushes and looks away. The old woman laughs and pats her on the arm.

"Aww, you two look cute together," the woman says. "How long have you two been dating?"

"Uh, a day?" I say. I'm not going to lie to the lady. I'm a lot of things, but I'm not a liar. "Give or take."

She laughs again, a fully body one. Yeah, I guess it's kind of amusing, huh?

"That's the right attitude to have, young man," she says. "Treat every day like it's your first. Keep the love and romance between you two alive."

"Yeah," I say. "I'll definitely do that, ma'am. Promise."

She starts to rise from the seat. She's older than she looks, or she's got some health problems. Slow and frail. I feel kind of bad now. Yeah, so, I'm kind of a prick sometimes, definitely an asshole other times, but I don't want to ruin some elderly lady's day or anything. I offer her my arm and help her up, then I go with her over to my old seat. I even carry her bag for her. It's not that heavy. It's the least I can do. I could probably lift her up and carry her over to the seat, but I'm pretty sure she'd slap me and beat me with her purse. I've seen that kind of thing happen in movies. My life's already fucked up enough as it is, I don't need to add anymore disaster.

The woman sits in my old seat and smiles at me.

"Hey," I say to the guy. "It was nice knowing you, but here's your new seat partner. She's nice. Don't mess with her, alright?"

The guy chuckles and the old woman grins.

"If he causes you any problems, you let me know," I tell her.

"Oh, I most certainly will," the old lady says, winking. They both introduce themselves and I let them be. Yeah, she'll be fine. They both seem like good people. I have no idea who they are, but I like them.

And now, I have a date. My first date. You ever been on an airplane for your first date? Me either. Kind of fucked up if you ask me. You think I'm going to get lucky at the end of this one? Maybe just a kiss, or will we go all the way? I hear girls love it when you get them a tiny package of mixed nuts, a can of soda, and an inflight movie. Romantic as fuck.

I go back to Ashley. She's watching me this time, not looking out the window. A stewardess up front is giving me the evil eye, but I ignore her. I'm going, lady. Give me two seconds. I sit in my seat and buckle up.

Ashley confronts me, hands on her hips, which looks a little funny considering she's sitting in an airplane seat. Now *she's* giving me the evil eye. What the fuck is up with this? What did I *just* do? It's like I didn't just help some old lady to her seat. That's a nice thing to do, isn't it? I really should get some bonus points for that. See? I'm not a complete asshole. Fuck.

Ashley just keeps grumping at me, though. Pouty lips. Holy fuck, she looks kissable right now. Probably more, but we're on an airplane. It's not like I can molest her right now, even though I kind of want to.

"When did I even agree to date you?" she asks.

"Wow. Seriously? I saved your ass and you're dumping me already?" I shake my head side to side and sigh.

"I can't dump you," she says. "We aren't even dating. Also, how's this going to work? We can't date, Ethan. It's only supposed to be a week. That's rule number one."

"Fuck rule number one," I say. "What rule are we on now? I forget."

"Sixteen," she says. "Or nine."

"I have no idea how that works. Is this some kind of calculus problem? Listen, Princess, I'm not great at math. Give me a break."

She punches me. Wow, she really is getting feisty. Who'd have thought it?

"It's not a math problem," she says. "I was thinking about it before, and I realized we never made a rule number nine. The last rule was number fifteen, though. Does that mean we just keep going to sixteen or do we have to have a rule number nine, too?"

"Nobody likes nine," I tell her. "Fuck rule number nine, too. It's almost as bad as rule number one. I'm striking it from the records."

"Oh, very official, Mr. Ethan Colton. Are you a judge now?"

"Yeah," he says. "And I'm declaring rule number sixteen right now. Rule number one is null and void. Over and done with. Get it the fuck out of here. I'm asking you out right here and now."

"What if I say no?" she says.

There's people looking at us. They probably think we're crazy. They'd probably think we were crazy if they realized Ashley's my stepsister. Do I look like I give a fuck, though? Nah, I don't care. Screw them.

"We had some other rule, too," I say. "Remember? The lying one. No lying to me, Princess. You can't say no, because we both know you want to say yes."

"I *would* like to say yes," she says. "That's true. I just... um... I really don't think it's a good idea. How is this going to work?"

"Fuck if I know. We'll figure it out together. We have the entire plane ride to do it."

"He's going to tell them anyways," she says. "That's... Ethan, that's why I went. Jake is going to tell them. They'll know. They probably already know."

"I don't care," I say. "Come here."

She does. We're both buckled in, thankfully, because when some stewardess passes by, she looks like she's going to freak out if we're not. We are, though. She gives us a strange look, then goes on her way. I don't care. Ashley's with me now, and she's cuddled close. The seat divider between us is lifted up and pushed into the seats between us, and she's leaning against me. I put my arm over her shoulder and hold her close.

"Don't you ever do something like that again, though," I tell her. "I get it. I really do. I know why you did it, but you don't have to do something like that. You should have told me."

"Sorry," she mumbles, looking down and away from me.

"You don't have to apologize, Princess," I say, reaching to lift her chin up.

I kiss her on the forehead, then the nose, and finally her lips. The last kiss lingers a little. I love the way her eyelashes flutter when I kiss her, like she's blinking away the brightness of the sun or something. It's beautiful.

"Everyone makes mistakes," I say. "It happens. Whatever. I'm not going to lose sleep over it. I'll still come rescue you again. I won't leave you like that."

"Do you think this is a mistake?" she says.

"Do I think what's a mistake?"

"This," she says again. "Us, I mean. What we're doing?"

"Nah," I say. "I've never been more sure of anything in my entire life."

It's true, too. I don't know when it happened. I didn't think it'd ever happen. I just... yeah... I don't want to lose her. It's as simple as that. Nah, that's not even it, it's not even simple. I *can't* lose her. I can't even imagine losing her. It's like an impossibility, except it almost happened, too.

I just kind of hope she feels the same way, too. Yeah, I'm a cocky, arrogant asshole, and I'm sort of a prick, but when I put my all into something, when I give it everything I've got, body, heart, and soul, I mean it. This isn't some fling. I don't want to fuck around and have a little fun. I'm in it for the long haul.

Yeah, maybe that's fucked up. This is my stepsister, you know? I never asked for that. I never even wanted it. I'm not going to blame my dad for falling in love. I hope he's not going to blame me for doing the same thing.

We cuddle the rest of the way home. Ashley falls asleep on my shoulder. Yeah, I'm tired, too. Shit, we've both been awake since nearly three in the morning. She woke up even earlier than me. I don't know about her, but I couldn't sleep on the plane ride to go get her. It was impossible. I kept thinking of everything bad that could happen, as if everything bad hadn't already happened.

This day started out bad. For all I know, it's going to be worse when we get home.

It's got to get better sometime, though. Tomorrow's a new day, too. Right?

Fuck, I hope so.

Mia Clark

11 - Ashley

Hey, Princess, wake up."

No, I don't want to wake up, I'm sleeping. I nuzzle against Ethan's shoulder and lift my chin up so I can kiss him on the cheek. That's what I meant to do, but it's a delightful surprise when my lips press against his lips instead. My eyes flutter open and see him there, so close to me. His eyes are very bright. I don't know if I've ever realized how bright his eyes are before. I want to keep looking into them forever.

"We're here," he says. "Time to go home."

"Home?" I ask, my voice rough from lack of use. I cough to clear my throat. "What do you mean?"

He rolls his eyes and grins at me, then looks all around. I follow his gaze.

Oh. Um... we're in an airplane. I almost forgot. It's not like I really ever intended for this to happen, though. I shouldn't be in an airplane right now.

I never should have left. I shouldn't have done what Jake wanted me to do. I should have told Ethan. I probably should have told my mom, too. I'm not sure about Ethan's dad. I don't know if I can tell him something like this. I hope Ethan can, though.

Then what, though? What's going to happen to us? Is this going to be alright? Are we going to be fine?

The plane is here and it's time for us to get out, so I guess we're about to find out what happens next. I'm scared. I feel like this is the hard part.

"Here, I'll take your bag," Ethan says.

"No, I can--" I start to say, but he takes it from me anyways. "Hey!"

He smirks and stands and shoulders my bag, then holds his hand out to me. "Come on, let's go. You hungry?"

"Yes," I say.

"You want to stop somewhere on the way? Get something to eat? We can sit down or do carry out and bring it home. Could just order something at home or make some food there, too. Whatever you want."

"I don't know if we have a home anymore," I tell him, truthful. "Ethan, Jake definitely told our parents by now. I really doubt they're going to be happy about this."

"Nah," he says. "It's fine. I'll deal with it."

It sounds nice, but... "You can't," I say. "It's not just your problem to deal with. We're going to have to deal with it together."

"Yeah, I guess so," he says, smiling. "After we eat, though."

"I doubt they're going to wait until we eat," I say.

"You need to stand up for yourself more," he says. "If you're hungry, you need to tell everyone else to fuck off until you've had a chance to eat."

"Oh, is that it?" We're walking down the aisle to the front of the plane now. Ethan must have let me sleep a little while even after we landed, because we're two of the last people on the plane. "You make everything sound so easy. I don't think it's as easy as you always seem to think."

"I never said anything is easy," he says. "If you're hungry, you should eat, though. What's the point in getting angry and starting an argument with someone for no reason when you could just sit down, eat some food, feel better, and then try to talk things through."

"I just don't think this is anything we can talk through," I say. "Do you really think that's going to work?"

"Sure," he says. "Why not?"

"Um, do you even realize what's been going on?"

A stewardess at the front of the plane waves and says goodbye to us. The pilot is there, too. He smiles and nods. Ethan waves back to the both of them. I give them a shy nod and mumble a good-bye. We step out into the gate exit and head to the airport interior. Everything seems a lot brighter here than I remember it being. Granted, when I was here earlier, it was dark out, but it still seems different. I'm not sure if we're in the same place. No, it's not that; I'm not sure if we're the same people.

I don't know if this is where I belong anymore.

"Cheer up, buttercup," Ethan says, nudging my side. "Don't look so glum, chum."

"Do you really think we have time to rhyme?" I ask.

"You just did it, too, snickerdoo."

"Snickerdoo isn't even a word!"

"Sure it is. I just made it up. What about those cookies?"

"Snickerdoodles?" I ask. "Those are good. We should get some."

Ethan laughs. "Is that it? Cookies make you happy? Shit, I'll get us a million. You'll never be sad for the rest of your life."

"Other things make me happy, too!" I say in protest.

"Oh yeah? Like what?"

"Um, sex is..." Oh my God, did I just say that? Start to say that... I didn't finish it. I can pretend I didn't.

"Cookies and sex?" Ethan asks. "Fuck yeah. I'm in. Let's go get to work."

"I hate how you're so casual about all this," I say.

"Nah," he says. "We were casual before, remember? I'm serious now. This is my serious face."

"Your serious face is really dumb," I say.

"Wow. Thanks a lot, Princess. What did I ever do to you?"

A lot. He's done a lot to me. So much. Maybe too much. I like all of it, though. Maybe I shouldn't, but I do.

"Let's just go home," I say.

"Yeah," Ethan says, smiling. "Let's do that."

Mia Clark

12 - Ethan

YEAH, WHATEVER. I get where she's coming from. I'm not exactly excited at what we're about to do, but we've got to do it anyways, so why worry about it? I don't like being scared. I tried being scared once. You know how fun that was? Not fun at all. Really sucked, actually. Kind of pissed me off. Never planning on doing that again. Let's just live life and see how it goes.

I get it, though. I'm not sure if we can even do that anymore. Thankfully we both have scholarships to fall back on. For awhile, at least. What happens after that?

My dad might disown me. He's a cool guy, and I don't hate him, but I'm not going to get upset at him if he's ticked off with me fucking my stepsister. It's not just that, either. Dating her? I feel like maybe that's almost worse than just having sex with her in secret. It's a lot harder to secretly date someone, especially if you want to hold their hand in public.

Whatever. I'll deal with it.

I don't know about her mom, either. I have no fucking clue how this is going to go. Maybe we'll have to move. Do you think we're going to be allowed to sleep down the hall from each other? Because, yeah, you know how that's going to end? Not well. I can try and pretend I'll be some holy saint, but I can all but assure you that every chance I get, I'll be sneaking into her room, or sneaking her into my room, and I'll be slamming my cock into her tight fucking beautiful gorgeous pussy as hard and as often as I can.

It's not just the sex, though. Yeah, sex is nice. I like it. Everyone should like sex. If you don't like it, there's something wrong there. Find a new partner? I don't know.

There's more, too, though. She's fun to hang out with. She's fun to talk to. I want to know more about her. I want to understand all the little shit. What's her favorite food? Her favorite cookie? What are her hopes and dreams and goals? Can I help? Can we do it together, or at least support each other?

Who knows? I sure don't. I want to find out, though.

We take a cab home. That part's easy. We sit in the back, quiet, and the driver drives. I don't know him. No clue who he is. I reach over and take Ashley's hand in mine and squeeze it. She looks over at me and smiles. Once we get back home, we go through the side door of the front gate and head to the front door of the mansion.

I open the door and lead the way inside. Maybe I should have been a gentleman and let her go first, but I doubt a real gentleman would let a lady walk headlong into the dungeon of a dragon like that, either. Because, yeah, that might be what we're walking into right now. We'll find out soon.

"It's quiet," she says. "Are they here?"

I shrug. "I don't know." Louder, shouting through the halls, I yell, "Hey, anyone home?"

Nothing. No one answers.

"They could be outside?" she says. "In the pool?"

"Yeah, maybe," I say. "Let's go check."

I walk through the place like I own it. I guess I kind of do. For now, at least. This is still my home until my dad disowns me, kicks me out, and cancels all of my credit cards and empties my trust fund account. That'll be a lot of fun to deal with.

Yeah, no one's out back, either. Ashley hovers behind me, like she's scared of leaving my side. I doubt she has to worry about much, though.

I'm the bad boy here. She's always been a good girl. I'll take the blame if I need to. It'll be easy for everyone to buy that, too. Oh, it's just Ethan being Ethan, fucking shit up. When's he going to stop being an idiot? When's he going to start being responsible? Ethan, Ethan, Ethan.

I don't know. I couldn't tell you. Maybe tomorrow. Maybe I already am. Maybe I never will be. Who knows?

"There's a note," Ashley says, pointing to the dining room table. "Two notes."

I head to the table and she follows along behind me again. It's cool. I'll protect you, Princess. Don't worry about it. And, yeah, there's two notes. One's for me and one's for her. Both are folded in half, crisp and clean. I recognize my dad's handwriting on mine. Ashley's mom wrote her note. I hand her hers and take mine, then open it and start reading.

This might be really bad. My dad couldn't even stand to see me, so he wrote a note to tell me to get the fuck out instead? Harsh.

Nah, that's not it. That's not what this note says at all. It's pretty regular and boring, to be honest. Nice note, though.

Hey,

Sorry to do this to you. I know we just got back, but there were some complications with one of the sites, and me and your stepmom had to take off again. We should have just stayed there for the rest of the week like we originally planned, but I thought we had everything sorted out. We'll be back in a few days, though.

Hey, Ethan? I know we don't talk on the phone much, but give me a call, alright? Let's figure out that camping trip I talked with you about before. I know we don't talk about it much, and I know I wasn't exactly there for you after, but when your mom died, it hurt. It's been so long, but it feels almost like it was yesterday, and I thought I was the one who hurt the most, but I never realized how much it must have hurt for you, too.

I'd like to start over again, though. I know things between us have been better these past few years, but that's no excuse. I don't want to ignore what I did. I want you to know I'm sorry, and I hope you can forgive me.

I know Ashley's mom isn't your real mom, but I hope you can still think of her as a mother. She cares about you, too. She says we should all have a family talk sometime soon, since we probably have a lot to talk about. I think I agree with her. How about we do it on our camping trip? It'd be nice to get away for awhile.

Not sure where you went off to so early this morning. Your stepmom said it was important and you had to go. I laughed, though. You? Important? When has that ever happened?

I hope it is, though. I hope you've found something important in your life. Whatever it is, I support you. You're a great kid, Ethan. I know you're an adult now, but you'll always be my son, too. I want what's best for you.

Take it easy while we're gone. Don't trash the house. Don't fight with Ashley too much. It's more trouble than it's worth. If she's anything like her mother, she's probably always right, anyways. Might as well just give in and listen to her.

Talk to you soon,
Dad

P.S. Can you pick some milk up at the store? We're running low. Thanks.

Well, I have no idea what the fuck this is, but it doesn't sound like a note from someone who knows I'm fucking my stepsister. Dating her, too. The dating thing just came up, though. We weren't dating before. I'm not even sure if we're dating now. She's being stubborn. I'll have to do a better job of convincing her.

Shit, this is hard. How do you convince a girl to date you? I usually do a lot of things with my cock, and that seems to work out most times, but I feel like maybe I'm going to have to change up my game soon. Fuck. What else is there? Uh... fancy restaurants? Oh, I bet that's it. You have to do nice things, and then the cock comes into play afterwards. So it's "ask her to a nice restaurant for dinner" and then "bang the shit out of her when we get home."

Right? Somebody help me out here. How's this work?

I turn to Ashley. Might as well ask her what's up. She's smart. Maybe she knows how this dating thing goes? I smile and start to crack some remark about us dating but...

She's crying. What did I do now? I didn't mean to, I swear. Fucking hell.

"What's wrong?" I ask.

Mia Clark

13 - Ashley

WHILE ETHAN READS HIS NOTE from his dad, I read the one from my mom. It's not normal. I'm not sure if any of this is normal. I don't know if I can ever go back to being normal.

Ashley,

I know what happened. I don't know everything about all of it, but I know enough. I hope you'll tell me the rest soon? I'd really like to know all the details, and I think we have a lot to talk about. I told your stepdad that we should have a family talk soon, but I didn't tell him why. It's up to you if you want to, though.

I know about you and Ethan, though. I'd be stupid not to. I wasn't sure at first what was going on. I thought maybe it was just a phase. I thought you two might be experimenting, and there's nothing wrong with that. Ethan is a little rough around the edges, but I know he wouldn't hurt you. If it's just a fling, I hope you won't get hurt, though. He has a bad habit of that.

I have reason to believe that's not it, though. Why else would my stepson go chasing after my daughter at an insane hour in the morning? Please believe me when I tell you that he was chasing after you, too. You should have seen him run out the door this morning. I'm not sure I've ever seen him do anything that fast and with such a determined look in his eyes. It was impressive!

I guessed what was going on when I saw you two together in your bed, though. I was even more sure about it when you asked if he could sleep in your room last night. I know that you've had feelings for him for a long time, but we stopped talking about that once I married his father, didn't we? I wasn't sure if you grew out of it and realized he wasn't the person for you, or if something else happened. I didn't want to pry.

All I can say is that you should follow your heart, wherever that leads you. I know it can hurt sometimes, and it can be hard, but I've done it twice now and I don't regret any of it. Your father was the love of my life at one time. I didn't think I'd find someone like that ever again, but then I met your stepfather, and it was love all over again. Neither one is stronger or weaker than the other, they're just different.

I hope you don't have to have two, though. I want you to be happy. If being happy means that you're with Ethan, then I think that's wonderful. If not, that's alright, too. I don't want you to make decisions based on what you think I'll think, though. I'm telling you right now that I won't think anything of it. No, that's not true. I'll be happy as long as you're happy. That's all that matters to me.

I'd like to ask you to please not go too crazy, though. I understand you're young, and so is Ethan, and he's got something of a reputation. Maybe you two will want to have sex? Maybe you already have? I'll talk to you about it if you want, but I'd like to not accidentally end up walking in on you both. That's bound to be awkward, because we all live together.

He has my permission to sleep in your room as often as he likes, though. I saw you when you were sleeping and you put your arms around him. It was slightly confusing at first, but you had the sweetest and most lovely expression on your face that I've ever seen. I can only describe it as seeing you truly happy. I hope that's what you are, too.

I don't mind seeing you two together like that, but I'd prefer if we could keep it like that with both of you wearing clothes. Lock your door if you want to do more. Also, try not to be too loud? I don't know if that's going to be an issue.

Don't forget your birth control, either. If you need anything else, you know where to find me.

Call me when you get back in. Me and your stepdad had to go back to the business site because of some complications, but we'll be back soon. He wants us to go camping when we get back. Wouldn't that be fun? I don't think we've ever gone camping before.

I don't know what happened between you and Jake, either, but if he tried to hurt you, let me know. I've never castrated anyone before, but there's a first time for everything, right?

Talk to you soon, honey.

Love,
Mom

I start to cry. I don't know why I'm crying, but I can't stop. I should have told her. I should have told her everything. She already knew? I'm not sure if she really did, but I bet she fully realized it when Ethan came to get me. I can understand how that might change someone's mind.

I've never had someone do that for me before, either. I didn't know something like that was possible. My mom and I have always been there for each other, but I thought that was because we're family. I didn't know that someone else could care about me so much that...

That he would call in a favor through his father's contacts and get my flight delayed, or that he would fly all the way to where I was going just to bring me right back, that he would save me from myself, that he would understand my mistakes and flaws and not care that I did something that was stupid.

Maybe he understands better than I thought, too. Ethan does a lot of stupid things, doesn't he? I wonder if they're really stupid, though, or if he does them for a reason. I don't think he's stupid. I never have, even though he acts strangely sometimes. He's acted that way since the second grade, and I didn't know why at first, but I found out later.

Maybe I forgive too easily. I don't think so, though. Not this time.

"What's wrong?" Ethan asks.

I hold out the note for him to read. I don't know how to explain it all. He reads and I sniffle. He's not done reading yet, but he comes closer to me and puts a hand on my hip, pulling me close to him. I go and nuzzle against him, holding him tight.

"Your mom is funny," he says, smiling. "You think she's really going to castrate him?"

I stop crying for a second, but only because I'm laughing now. "That's what you got out of that note?" I ask. "Really, Ethan!"

"Hey, sometimes you've got to look on the bright side, Princess."

I smile a little. Ethan reaches out and wipes the tears from my cheeks. He puts the note on the table and leans down to kiss the rest of the tears from my eyes, too.

"Is everything alright with your dad?" I ask.

"Yeah, sure," he says. "We'll figure it out."

I don't like how he says that. "What's that mean?"

Ethan shrugs. "He doesn't know yet, but I think he'll understand."

"Oh. Are you sure?"

"Yeah, I'm pretty sure," he says. "Hey, I've got to make a phone call, though. Do you mind?"

"Um... no? Who are you calling?"

"It's a secret," Ethan says with a grin. "Top secret super secret. I'll let you listen in if you want, though."

I roll my eyes at him. He's just so weird sometimes. I like it, though. We head to the living room. He's going to use the house phone. A red light under the base of the phone is blinking, too. We have a message to listen to, apparently. Ethan furrows his brow and picks up the phone, then presses the button to start the message through the speaker.

It's Jake. I recognize his voice immediately.

"This message is for Ashley's mom and Ethan's dad. I'll call back later because I was hoping to talk to you both in person, but I need you to know what's going on first, too. There's no easy way to say this, but your daughter and son have been having sex together. Yes, I know this is gross and disturbing, because they're practically brother and sister, but I have undeniable proof. If you can get back to me with a number that I can text you at, or an email address, I'll be happy to forward everything I have to you, too."

"Wow," Ethan says. "What a dick, huh?"

"Um, that's an understatement," I say, tensing up a little. Ethan squeezes me close to him, calming me.

Jake continues.

"I'm sorry to be the one to tell you this, but you really should know. I tried to talk with Ashley about it, but I think maybe Ethan is abusing her and forcing her to stay quiet. It's possible she's innocent in all of this, but I doubt it. Did you know she's been sending him naked pictures? It's incredibly easy for these things to get leaked on the internet nowadays, too. I hope you won't take this the wrong way, but I'd be happy to fully destroy the evidence I have for a small price, too. I wouldn't think of this as a bribe, but more of the cost for removing all traces of what's been going on."

"Why the fuck did you date this guy again?" Ethan asks.

"I thought he was nice, Ethan! I don't know!"

"How long do you think it'll take me to fly back there? I don't think I punched him in the face enough. Should probably do it a couple more times just to make sure I did it right."

I roll my eyes and laugh. This situation isn't funny. Far from it. It's just that Ethan has a way of making things seem less serious than they are. I think that's what I need right now, though.

"You can call me back at this number," Jake finishes on the message, rattling off his cellphone number. "I know it's a difficult situation to take in at first, but I'd be happy to discuss it with you as best I can."

Without a second's hesitation, Ethan deletes the message.

"You deleted it!" I say, shocked. "Ethan!"

"What?" he says, giving me a funny look. "What the hell was I supposed to do with it?"

"I don't know. I don't think you were supposed to delete it, though."

"The stupid fuck is just going to call back and leave more messages. Who cares?"

"He said he's going to put my picture on the internet," I say. "I don't think I like that."

Ethan shrugs. "It's just your body from the shoulders down. It's not like anyone can see your face."

"Oh, so that makes it fine? You want random people on the internet to see me naked?"

"Nah, but it's not as bad as it could be," he says. "Here, I'll make it up to you. You can take a picture of me naked from the shoulders down, and then post it on the internet or whatever you want. Sound good?"

"Not really."

"Wow, you're hard to please, huh?"

"Can I take pictures of you naked and not post them on the internet?"

"Whoa, getting kinky there, Princess," he says, smirking. "I like it. Let's do it."

I groan and roll my eyes. "You're weird."

"Yeah yeah. Hey, hold on I've got a phone call to make."

He dials a number on the phone and waits for someone to pick up. I watch him, waiting and listening. This is top secret super secret. It must be important.

"Yeah, hey," he says into the phone. "Can we get a delivery? Yeah, uh... alright. Whoa, that's your special for the day? Yeah, send that. Side of french fries, too. You got anything fancy? Toppings or something? Shit, yeah, that sounds good. Subs, too. Steak and cheese? Two. Got it. Everything. Yeah. Pickles and mayo, too. How much is that? Yeah, I'll pay with a card." He says the number for a credit card without even bothering to look at one. He memorized it? Wow. "Alright, but hey, it's a mansion. There's a gate. It's easier if the delivery guy calls me and I head out to get it. He can hit the buzzer, too. Whatever works. Yeah, thanks a lot."

Ethan hangs up the phone. I stare at him, dumbfounded. He looks back at me like I'm crazy.

"What's with the face?" he asks.

"I thought you said you had an important call to make," I say. "You just called a pizza place. I'm hungry, too, but I don't think that's important."

"Fuck you," he says. "Steak and cheese subs are important as fuck. You know what they've got on them? Mushrooms, green peppers, onions, bacon, and pickles and mayo, too. You don't even understand, Princess. You will, though. Once he gets here, you're going to feel bad for ever doubting me."

"What, bacon?" I ask. "Is that really on them? That sounds amazing."

"Shit, wait until you see the pizza! They're trying some new thing. You'll love it."

"I'm still not sure this is very important," I say, scrunching up my nose and glaring at him.

"Whatever," he says. "Fine. Hold on. I'll make another call."

Oh, great. Who is he calling now? Someone stupid, probably. I wish he would take this--

"Yeah, uh, hey, this is Ethan? Your stepson. Are you busy?"

--seriously... did he just call my mom?

"Alright. Cool. Yeah. Can I put you on speakerphone. Ashley's here, too."

He nods into the phone. A second later he hits the button to put it on speakerphone.

"Hi, Ashley," my mom says through the phone. "Are you alright?"

"Um... yeah, mom. I'm fine. We just got back."

"Glad to hear it," my mom says. "Ethan wants to talk to me, I guess. Is everything alright, Ethan?"

"Yeah," he says. "Just uh... hey, I've never done this before, so go easy on me, alright?"

My mom laughs. "Sure. What is it, honey?"

"Oh, is my dad there, first?"

"No. Do you want to wait? He's in a meeting right now. I'm in the hotel room by myself. Is that alright?"

"Yeah, that's probably better. This doesn't really involve him. Not yet. I'll talk to him later."

"Alright," my mom says. I can sense her grinning on the other end of the phone. Ethan is being more than a little vague.

"Yeah, so..." Ethan starts to say, then hesitates. "Look, I get that this is kind of fucked up, and I won't be upset if you just tell me that, but I'd really like to date your daughter, and I hope you'll let me. I've never done this before, but I thought I should be a real gentleman about it. Chivalrous as fuck, right?"

"Ethan, I'm not sure real gentleman swear so much," my mom says.

"Yeah, I told you I've never done this before. Cut me some slack?"

"So you want to date my daughter, though?" my mom asks. "Why should I let you?"

Now she's just teasing him! No one is taking this seriously, are they? This is serious. My God!

"You probably shouldn't," Ethan says. "I'm kind of an asshole and mostly a prick. I really like her, though. I've never felt this way about a girl before. Kind of fucked up, huh?"

"Ethan, did you know that Ashley used to come home from school when she was in second grade and she would tell me about this boy she met. He was really nice to her at first, but then he went away for a week, and after that he looked sad. That's exactly what she said. Also, after that, she told me that he used to flip her skirt up. I asked her if she wanted to start wearing pants to school instead, but she told me no, that she would just hold her skirt down and stop him."

Ethan grins and tosses me a sidelong glance.

"Excuse me!" I say, grabbing for the phone. "Why are we talking about this?"

Ethan dodges and lifts the phone out of my reach. He's too tall! Argh! I try to jump up and grab it, but he holds me at bay.

"Yeah, that never worked," Ethan says, loud enough so my mom can hear it. "I was kind of a troublemaker back then."

"You still are, honey," my mom says, laughing. "I don't know if Ashley will ever tell you this, so I'm going to, though. I think she's been in love with you, at least a little bit, since second grade, and I think that love has grown since then, too. She tells me everything, and while she never said that she loved you, your name has come up in a lot of our conversations."

"Mom!" I shout. "That's not true!"

It is true. Why am I denying it? I don't know.

"I'm fine with you dating my daughter, Ethan. You've both known each other for longer than your father and I have known each other, and maybe you've both loved each other a little bit longer than I've loved your father, too. I'm going to talk with him, alright? It might be difficult at first, but I think we can all figure this out. I hope we can start once we get back, too. I think it'd be a lot of fun to go camping together, don't you? You're both important to me, no matter what happens."

I stop trying to grab the phone away from Ethan. There's no point anymore. I just want to know one thing, though.

"Mom, why are you doing this? Why are you saying all of this? You don't think it's... it's gross or anything?"

"Your daughter sure knows what to say to make a guy feel good," Ethan says.

My mom laughs. "Ashley, no, it's not gross. It's a little strange, yes, but sometimes we're all strange, aren't we? Just please promise me you won't have sex in the hot tub. It's hard to clean that out."

"Mom!" I shout, grabbing for the phone again. "Seriously?"

"Yeah uh, sorry," Ethan says, all while dodging away from me. "Not to give you too much information here, but we kind of already did that."

"Ethan!"

"I'm hanging up now!" my mom says. "I'm going to pretend I didn't hear that! I hope you two have a nice time. Don't go too crazy, please. I want to come home to a house that's all in one piece. Bye, Ashley. Bye, Ethan."

I stop to say bye to my mom, because it just seems like the right thing to do?

"Bye, Mom."

Ethan says it, too. "Bye, Mom." There's a click and my mother hangs up the phone.

"Gross," I say. "Did you have to call her that, too?"

"What, she's my mom now? You got a problem with that, Princess?"

"You're disgusting," I say.

"Look, I didn't want to be the one to bring this up, but you're the one who started calling me 'brother' right in the middle of sex the other night. What the fuck was up with that?"

"I was trying to annoy you!" I say. "You know what, though? It just made you harder. I felt it, Ethan. You were inside me. You're a huge pervert, aren't you?"

"Yeah, so what? You're not any better."

"Nyah!" I... say. Is that something someone can say? I stick my tongue out at him, anyways.

"Just don't do it again, you fucking freak."

"I'll do whatever I want to do," I say, making a face at him. "I'm not a freak, you are."

"You want me to show you what kind of freak I can be, Princess? Are you forgetting we're alone in the house again for the next few days? You don't want to start shit you can't finish. For real."

"I can finish anything," I say. "You're the one who causes trouble, Ethan. I have perfect grades."

"Oh yeah? I'll grade you, alright. You get an F for that fuckable little pussy of yours. Get the hell over here so I can take advantage of it."

"You're going to take advantage of me!" I say, eyes wide, trying not to laugh.

"Damn straight," he says, grinning and trying not to laugh, too.

The phone starts to ring. Ethan still has it in his hand. He pushes a button to pick up the call and practically roars into the phone.

"Who the fuck is--" But then he stops and calms down. "Oh, hey. Yeah, sorry man. You're here? Cool, I'm starving. I'll be right out."

"Pizza?" I ask.

"Yeah," Ethan says, smirking. "You're safe for now, Princess. Once we're done eating, your pussy is mine, though. Don't you forget it."

"If we're going to be dating, you have to be a little more romantic than that," I say.

"Shit," he says. "This is difficult, isn't it?"

14 - Ethan

E THAN?" Ashley says.

"Yeah, what's up?" I ask.

"I need to stop eating. Everything is delicious but I need to stop."

"What the hell? You didn't even eat all of your sandwich. There's half still there." Yeah, I'm done mine. It was the first thing I ate, though. You think I'm going to let a steak and cheese sub sit around uneaten? You're crazy.

"I'll eat it later," she says. "I'm going to save it. I can't eat anymore now, though."

"I'll eat it," I say. "Hand it over." I hold out my hand, making this easy for her.

"What? No! It's mine."

"You just said you aren't going to eat it."

"I didn't say that. I said I would eat it *later*," she says.

"It's not even the same," I tell her. "A cold steak and cheese sub? What's with that?"

"I can heat it up in the microwave, you know?" She looks at me like I'm the crazy one here.

"Not as good," I tell her. "Maybe if you put it in the oven it'll be alright, but it's going to dry out, too. Shouldn't you know this stuff? I thought you were the smart one."

"Wow," she says, slapping playfully at my arm. "If you want to keep dating me, you should try and be a little nicer."

"What for?" I ask, grinning.

She shrugs. "I don't know. Because?"

I laugh and move closer to her. We're on the couch. Yeah, not the best place to eat, especially with all the food we have, but whatever. Our parents are gone, so it's cool, right? They'll never know. Except Ashley's a klutz and dropped some steak on the couch, smearing grease all over the place. It's a leather couch, too. I guess that makes it a little easier to wipe up, but I have no idea if it's going to leave a stain or not. We'll find out soon enough.

"Listen," I tell her. "I'm going to tell you some secrets right now, specially reserved for you. I don't just tell this kind of stuff to everyone, though. You're the first."

She brightens up and keeps her eyes locked on mine, intense and intent. "What? Really? What is it?"

"If you're dating someone, you don't take any shit from them, alright? If I try to steal your sandwich, you tell me to back the fuck off. Go ahead, try it. Stand up for yourself."

"Um... alright..."

I give her something to work with. "Hey, give me the rest of your sandwich, Princess. You're not eating it, right?"

"No, Ethan!" she says. It's loud, but the way she says it makes me laugh. "This is my sandwich. You... you back off!" She pauses for a second, then looks at me funny. "What are you laughing about? You told me to say it!"

"Nah, you did good," I say. "Good job. See? It's a mutual thing. Mutual respect here. Sometimes I might overstep my bounds or something. You never know, right? If I do, you just tell me, and I'll take a step back and realize what's up. I don't want you to be mad at me, Princess. If something I do makes you mad, or if I'm about to do something that'll make you mad, you tell me, alright?"

"Alright," she says, smiling. "You can have a bite of my sandwich if you want, though. It's a lot."

"Going back on your word already? What's up with that?"

"Shut up, Ethan! Take a bite of my sandwich, or else!"

She starts to giggle at me. Holy fuck, she's beautiful. And fun. Gorgeous and cute and amazing. Why is she with me? I don't even know. Am I the luckiest guy in the world or what? Probably.

She comes closer, grinning from ear to ear, and holds up the sandwich. I'm pretty sure she's got plans for something, but whatever. You think I can pass up a bite of a steak and cheese sub? Not at all. I open my mouth and take a bite, which goes fine, but at the last minute she moves it to the side quick, smearing mayo on my lips to my cheek.

"Whoops!" she says. Still grinning, also giggling.

"Yeah, whoops," I say, rolling my eyes at her. "What was that for--"

I find out soon enough. She puts the sub back on her plate and moves it to the coffee table, then she prowls across the couch on her hands and knees, crawling into my lap. She licks my cheek, cleaning the mayo from it, then closer to my lips. Then we kiss. She puts her arms around my neck and sits in my lap, kissing me. I kiss her back. You think I can pass up a chance at kissing her? Nah, never.

"What do people in relationships do?" she asks me after we take a break. Her arms are still around my neck and she's still sitting in my lap.

I grab her ass in my hands and squeeze it, pulling her closer. "I have no idea," I tell her. "I've never done this before."

"I kind of have," she says. "I guess. I'm not sure if I really did, though."

"I guess we'll have to figure it out," I say, shrugging. "What do you want to do?"

"Have sex," she says. "I want you to take your shirt off, too."

"Yeah, people in relationships definitely have sex," I tell her, snickering. "I'm sure there's a little more to it."

"We can go to the movies?" she says. Her hands move to the bottom of my shirt and she tugs it up.

I help her bring it all the rest of the way, lifting it up and over my head. "We can go on vacation together," I say. "Somewhere real nice. We could go to Europe or France or something."

"Ethan, France is in Europe. If we go to France, we're also going to Europe."

"Thanks for the geography lesson, Princess," I say, groaning. "I really appreciate it."

"I want to talk to you on the phone, too," she says. "We've never really talked on the phone before, you know?"

"What do you want to talk to me on the phone for? I'm right here."

"Not *now*," she says. "Later, I mean. Because um... we're going to be going back to school, aren't we? How's that going to work?"

"Fuck if I know," I say. Because, yeah, I have no idea. I didn't think that far ahead.

She frowns and pouts at me. It's kind of cute, but serious, too. This is an issue, isn't it? I can't fuck this up.

"I want it to work, though," I say. "Maybe we can visit each other on the weekends."

"Every weekend?" she asks, skeptical.

"Yeah, why not?" I think it's a pretty great plan, myself. "You come see me one weekend and I go see you the next weekend."

"That's going to be expensive," she says. "Do you think we can do that?"

"It's not that bad. An hour or two away? It'll be fine. Besides, my dad's rich. I hear your stepdad is rich, too."

She rolls her eyes at me and makes a face. "Your dad is my stepdad," she says. "It's not like there's two rich people involved here."

"He's got a billion dollars or something, so it's cool," I say, grinning.

"He doesn't know yet, though," she says. "Do you think he'll be alright with it?"

"I think so," I say. "I guess we'll find out soon, though."

"I'm kind of scared," she says.

"About what?"

"Us? This? Everything? How are we going to explain it to everyone? What if they think it's weird? I think it's kind of weird, myself."

"Yeah," I say. "I get that, Princess. I really do. It doesn't matter, though. Why do we have to tell anyone? It's not like they have to know."

"Eventually someone's going to find out," she says. "People are going to talk about it, and I don't know what to do about that."

"I do," I say, flexing for her. She giggles. It's cute as fuck. "I'll punch them. Anyone says anything bad and I'll kick their ass."

"You can't just punch people!" she says, laughing. "That's not the answer to everything. Also, what if it's a girl who says it?"

"Shit," I say. "In that case, you'll have to punch them. Yeah, that's it. We've got this covered, Princess. Don't worry."

She sighs and lays her cheek against my shoulder. "I'm not punching anyone. I don't want to."

"I guess you'll just have to ignore them, then," I say, wrapping my arms tight around her. I hold her close and hug her, feeling her warmth against my bare chest. "Hey, why am I the only shirtless one here by the way?"

"You want me to take my shirt off, too?" she asks. Is that excitement I see in her eyes? Mhm...

"I want you to take it all off," I say. "We can start with the shirt, though."

Everything starts somewhere. I've realized that over the past few days. I never really thought about it before, but yeah, everything starts somewhere. It might seem simple or stupid or innocent, but it might not be. It could be the start of something wonderful and beautiful, or dangerous and risky, or it could be the stupidest thing you've ever done in your entire life. It might be all of those things combined. You don't know until you do it.

I don't know when exactly *we* started, but I know when I pulled her shirt over her head. I know when I reached behind her and unclasped her bra, then tossed it to the floor. I might be able to tell you the exact moment when I looked down at her breasts and thought they were perfect. Maybe even when I leaned her back and bent my head down, taking her nipple in my mouth. Also, when she let out a gasp and her back arched even more when I scraped my teeth across her sensitive little nub.

That's how that started. It hasn't ended yet. I'm still going. She makes me so fucking hard I don't know if I can ever stop.

I grab her ass hard and stand up, holding her against me. Ashley laughs and shrieks, then clings to my neck, holding herself up. I step around the couch, leaving our food on the coffee table, and I carry her out of the living room and into the halls. Then up the stairs. At the top, I jerk my head to either side.

"Where to?" I ask. "Your room or mine?"

"Yours," she says, with love and lust in her eyes.

Yeah, that's where we go. I kick open my door and step to my bed, then toss her onto it. She falls and bounces on her back on my bed, her breasts swaying side to side. Sexy as fuck, that's what that is. I slam my door shut hard, then I'm on her. Pants, off. Socks and panties, gone. She's bare and on my bed and holy fuck she's mine.

"Do you remember what rule number eleven is?" I ask her.

She bites her lip and nods. "Do *you* remember what rule number eleven is? I didn't think you remembered any of the numbers."

"Nah, I remembered that one," I say. "Never going to forget it, either."

I grab her hips and pull her up, swinging her feet over my shoulders as I kneel down beside my bed. Then, yeah, *rule number eleven*. Fuck, she tastes amazing. The perfect dessert after an amazing meal. I slide my tongue up and down her slit, tasting her. She's wet already, and as soon as I touch my tongue to her sex, she lets out a sharp gasp and rolls her hips up to meet my mouth.

"Calm down there, Princess," I tell her, smirking. "I just started."

She doesn't answer with her words. Instead, she grabs the back of my head and pulls me against her crotch.

"You... you told me to tell you if you were doing something that made me upset," she says. "If you don't keep doing that right now, I'm going to be upset."

"Oh yeah?" I ask.

"Mhm."

Right, then. I can do that. I tease my tongue past her slick folds and dip it into her juicy center. She clenches her thighs against my head, making this more than a little difficult. I grab her thighs and pull them apart, giving me easier and better access. She starts to whimper and moan when I lap up and lick against the hood of her clit.

"I didn't think we'd ever do this again," she whispers. "I thought that after today we would—"

"You think too much," I tell her. "Rules are rules, though, Princess. As far as I remember, rule number eleven applies to every single day, so you better get used to this."

I slide my hand towards her center, and while I'm licking all around her clit, I tease a finger inside her. I can feel her clenching hard against me as I enter her. I slide it in, pressing against her inner walls, then I lick at the tip of her clit. She squirms and spasms on my bed, her whole body pulsing around me.

She's tight. Maybe that's a part of her magic. I don't know. Two fingers is her limit, though, and even that's a tight squeeze. I put another one inside her while focusing on the center of her pleasure. I can feel her getting closer now. This is it.

The secret to a woman's orgasm isn't just in the technique, either. It's about relaxation, about making her feel calm and comfortable. I shift one hand up and around her leg, towards her stomach, and flattening my palm against her pubis, just above her clit. It's safe, it's a protection thing. I've got her, she's not going anywhere, I'll protect her. Forever.

"I'm... I am, Ethan. Right--"

Now. Right this very second. She starts to cum. I can feel a surge of wet arousal coating my fingers. I lighten up on her clit, licking a little lower, giving her some space. Not too light, though. I just want her to feel good. I don't want to overload her with sensation and pleasure. Sometimes too much of a good thing really is too much. Also, we're going to have a lot of a good thing real fucking soon. I'm nowhere near done with her yet.

I think she knows this, too.

Even before she's calmed down from her climax, she's pulling me up. She pulls me towards her, lifts my head, pulls me to her face. She kisses me fast and reaches down to my hips, grappling with my pants.

"Please," she whimpers. "Ethan, I want you inside me. Please?"

"Your wish is my command, Princess."

It's not difficult. It's so fucking easy to take your pants off. I do that, and my underwear, too, then I climb up on the bed. I kiss her while I get into position between her legs. Her thighs wrap around my hips.

I don't even try. I don't have to. This is easy. It's like walking or breathing. Do you even think about it? No, it just comes natural. That's how this works, too. First, I'm outside her, and then I'm in, no thought involved, no confusion, nothing.

I push all the way inside her in one smooth motion. We're kissing, or we were, but now she's biting my bottom lip, her eyes screwed up and shut tight, a look of intense satisfaction on her face.

That's how it starts. Everything has to start somewhere, right?

15 - Ashley

I CAN FEEL ETHAN DEEP INSIDE ME. He's... he's large. Not too large, though. I think he's perfect. I haven't had a lot of sex before this, but this is perfect. It's always been perfect. I don't know how, but he knows exactly what to do and exactly when to do it. Stranger still, I feel like I know exactly what to do when I'm with him, too.

It's not just now, but always. It's always been always.

I remember that first night. Yes, I was a little buzzed, but I can still remember what happened. It felt perfect then, too. I remember having a slight feeling of guilt, because I was definitely aware that this was Ethan, this was my stepbrother, but even still, as soon as I felt him inside me, all misgivings about what we were doing drifted away.

After that, it became perfect. We felt perfect together. My body just... it knew. It knew exactly what to do with him, and exactly how to do it. I knew exactly how to feel. I'd never had an orgasm during sex before that. I hadn't ever really had an orgasm with anyone else before that in any capacity.

Now, though? Now I've had one every single time I've been with Ethan. Most of the time I've had more than one. I just had one, and now we're having sex, so...

He wraps his body around mine. It's a perfect fit, and we mold together perfectly. He pulls out of me, then thrusts back in, rough, yet knowing. Our bodies clash, fighting against each other, matched evenly, like rivals who have known each other for ages. Below us, Ethan's bed creaks, and I bounce atop his mattress with each of his thrusts.

"You feel so fucking perfect," he says. "It's insane how fucking good my cock feels when I'm inside you."

I laugh a little, but it's hard to think right now. "You're not supposed to say things like that, you bad boy."

"Oh yeah?" he says, grinning and leaning close to whisper into my ear. "You know what else? I want to feel you cum around my cock, Princess. I want to fill you, balls deep, while you can't help but keep cumming, and then I'm going to fill you the fuck up with my cum, too."

"That's not something a stepbrother should say to his stepsister!" I say, teasing, playful.

"Holy fuck, not that again," he says, grunting.

He's harder now, though. I don't know if it's because of the taboo nature of what we're doing, or if it's something else. I like how I can feel him harden and thicken and pulse and throb inside me, though. I can feel every inch of his cock moving as if it was a part of my own body. It's exhilarating and intoxicating and I love it.

"Fill me, Ethan," I moan into his ear. "Please, I need it."

"I'll fill you as soon as you--"

I can feel him holding off, his willpower straining against his body's needs. I don't, though. I don't hold off at all. My body gives in to him, with absolute completeness. My orgasm overtakes me. I clench my eyes shut and focus on every single feeling, all of the myriad sensations, his slick abs, wet with a mixture of our sweat, sliding up and down my stomach, my breasts squished beneath his torso, his teeth nibbling at my ear, his hips rocking against mine, his cock thrusting in and out of me.

Not out anymore, though, just in. I squeeze and climax, just like he wanted, milking his cock with every inch of my core. Ethan pushes hard into me, keeps pushing. His hips rock back and forth a little like he wants to go even further inside of me somehow, but it's physically impossible. The head of his cock grinds against my inner depths, goading me on to even higher peaks of passion.

He gives in, too. I thought my orgasm was wonderful and nice before, but it becomes ecstatic art as soon as I feel the warmth of his seed inside me. I can feel his cock throbbing, clenching, flexing hard like his abs, another muscle in need of a workout. I want Ethan to be my workout partner in this, too. I want to become strong with him, I want our relationship to grow powerful.

I know it's not just sex that makes a good couple, but I think we have everything else, also. He's my opposite, but not quite. He matches all of me. He complements my soul in a way I never thought possible. I know how to... how to *be* when I'm with him. It's strange to think of it like that, but it's true.

Before Ethan, I always felt subconscious about a lot of things. I wasn't sure if I was doing anything right. I didn't have a way to find out, either. Sometimes I would look things up on the internet or ask friends. Is this normal? What if I'm doing it wrong? I had questions about everything, because that's how I always was. You can study for a test and get perfect grades, but it's not as easy to study for a relationship.

I don't have to anymore, though.

Ethan collapses atop me as our bodies work against one another, fulfilling each other's desires. He breathes hard against my neck and I laugh and wrap my arms around him, holding him tight. He's heavy, though.

"Ethan, I can't breathe," I say, laughing. "Get up!"

"Fuck that," he says, grumbling and lifting himself off of me. "I just want to fall asleep on top of you and inside you. Is that too much to ask?"

"Here," I say. We shift and move up the bed, under the blankets. "Come here. We can cuddle and you can sleep on me like that."

I lay on my back and pull Ethan alongside me. I put one of his arms over my chest, and move his head to my shoulder. It's always the other way around, with me laying on him, but I think I like this, too.

"You came a lot, huh?" I say. "I can feel it."

"You know just what to say to wake me up, Princess," Ethan says, grinning. "Yeah, I had some pent up desires going on there or something. We haven't had sex for over a day."

"Oh, poor baby," I say, patting his cheek. "How did you survive?"

"I have no idea," he says, shaking his head. "I barely made it."

"What are you going to do when we go back to college?" I ask. "Even if we see each other every weekend, that'll be five days apart."

"Shit," he says. "It will, won't it? Fuck. Uh... the only way we can solve this problem is we're going to have to find a company that can make a mold of your pussy. Out of that sex toy stuff, right? Then you'll have to talk dirty to me on the phone while I fuck the shit out of the mold. It'll work."

"A mold? Do they even do that?"

"Yeah, sure, why not?"

"What about me, though?"

"You want a mold of my cock? Sounds kind of great, actually. You can show it off to your friends. Tell them how amazing I am."

"I'm not going to do that!" I say, laughing. "Wait, you can't do that, either. If you have a mold of... of me, you can't show it to anyone. That's just weird."

"Yeah, *that's* the weird part about all of this," he says. "Nothing else. I agree."

"You're a jerk," I say, slapping his shoulder.

"Whatever," he says. "You still love me."

I freeze. Love? Um... we haven't talked about this. I didn't know we were going to talk about this. It seems too soon? Except maybe not. Maybe it isn't at all.

"Sorry," Ethan says. "A little awkward. It just kind of came out."

"Did you mean it?" I ask. "I mean, do you love me, too?"

"Listen, Princess, I don't know if we should be having this conversation right now."

"Ethan," I say, steady and firm, but calm and loving. "I want to have this conversation. Right now. Please?"

He hesitates, then sighs. "Yeah," he says after awhile. "I think so. I love you."

"What do you mean you think so?" I ask. "What's that mean?"

"You know how your mom mentioned that you've loved me, at least a little bit, since the second grade?" he asks.

"Yup?"

"I didn't love you back then. We were what, like seven or something? But I liked you a lot. I've always really liked you, Princess. I remember getting pissed when we weren't in the same class during elementary school. Then when you were smarter than me and had higher level classes than me in high school, I was even more pissed. I was excited when I saw you trying out to be a cheerleader, since I thought I'd get to see you more after school, but that never happened."

"Why didn't you tell me?" I ask.

"Because," he says. "I'm not good for you. I wasn't good for you then. I don't even know if I'm good for you now. You're way too smart for me, for one. Also, I'm just kind of a jerk. I don't exactly mean to be, it just happens."

"Rule number seventeen can be you can't be a jerk to me," I say.

"To you?" he asks, smirking. "Just to you?"

"Mhm, just me," I say, smiling. "You can be a jerk to everyone else if you want, though. I don't think you should, but I don't think you are right now, anyways."

Ethan slides one hand down my stomach, to my sex. His fingers start to idly play with me there, just teasing me softly, caressing up and down, back and forth. I shiver at his touch and nuzzle closer to him.

"I want to be good for you, Princess. I don't want to be a mistake. I don't want you to regret this."

"Sometimes it might be hard," I say, closing my eyes, feeling him. Not just his fingers teasing me, but *him*; his thoughts and his hesitation. "A lot of the time it'll be nice, though."

"How do you know?" he asks, curious.

"I don't," I tell him. "I think it's true, though. Sometimes we can't always know the exact answer, but we need to give it our best shot, anyways. It's like an essay question on a test."

"Shit," he says, laughing. "I hate those ones the most. Where are the multiple choice questions?"

"Right here," I say, lowering my hand to touch against the back of his while he teases my labia with his fingers.

"Hey, I think I know the answer to that one," he says, his face lighting up, grinning.

"You do," I say, smiling and turning to kiss him.

"I do love you, Princess," Ethan says. "I'm just scared I'm going to fuck it up. I'm not good at loving anyone."

"It's hard to love," I say. "That's why you don't have to do it alone. I'll be your study buddy."

He laughs. "You're good at this."

"I love you, too. That's why."

We're quiet after that. Ethan smooths his hand up and away from my sex, along my stomach, towards my breasts. He touches my chin and moves to the side a little, propping himself up on his shoulder to give him easier access to kiss me. We kiss like that, soft and sweet, cute and nice.

He's my bad boy and I'm his good girl.

And, yes, he's my stepbrother and I'm his stepsister.

He wasn't always, though. We aren't just that. There's a lot more to us.

There's nothing wrong with what we're doing. I know other people will think so, but they're wrong. Sometimes you need to follow your heart, or else you'll regret it for the rest of your life. You don't always have a choice in who you fall in love with.

Sometimes you can't be perfect. You just have to be yourself. Sometimes that's what makes you perfect.

Ethan and I fall asleep in each other's arms. We wake up like that, too. It's different from all the other times, though. It's different because we don't have a time limit on our relationship anymore. We don't have to cram everything into just a week. We have a lot longer.

"Now you're my boyfriend," I say, "with benefits."

"Boyfriend with benefits?" he asks, grinning. "I like the sound of that."

"I love you, Ethan," I say.

He kisses me softly. "I love you, too, Princess. Thanks."

He doesn't tell me what he's thankful for, and I don't ask. I think I know already. I think I feel the same way.

A NOTE FROM MIA

YAY! THE STORY IS DONE! I hope you liked it as much as I enjoyed writing it.

While the story is over for now, I was actually considering adding more. I'd love your thoughts on that one. Kind of like a second season for Ashley and Ethan, that picks up where this one ends. My idea for that would be to write about the camping trip with Ashley and Ethan and their parents all together as um... a family, except maybe there's some problems going on, too?

I also have some bonus scenes that I'll be adding to the Cherrylily website soon, so if you'd like to know a little more about Ashley and Ethan's past, then you can read about it there. I'm still working on them, but you can email me at mia@cherrylily.com or follow me on Facebook at https://www.facebook.com/MiaClarkWrites to find out more about those. It's fun extra stuff, but I think you'll like it.

And that's it! I hope you enjoyed the story a lot, and I hope you'll keep an eye out for more of my books in the future.

If you like these books, I'd love if you rated and reviewed them. How did you like how it ended? Nice to see Jake get dealt with! Ethan is a little nicer than he first seemed, huh? I think Ashley is good for him, too. They both make each other better. I hope it works out for the in the future, though. Things might be hard, but together I think they can do it!

I hope you enjoyed reading about them, and I hope I'll see you around again for more of my books.

Thanks for reading!

~MIA

ABOUT THE AUTHOR

Mia likes to have fun in all aspects of her life. Whether she's out enjoying the beautiful weather or spending time at home reading a book, a smile is never far from her face. She's prone to randomly laughing at nothing in particular except for whatever idea amuses her at any given moment.

Sometimes you just need to enjoy life, right?

She loves to read, dance, and explore outdoors. Chamomile tea and bubble baths are two of her favorite things. Flowers are especially nice, and she could get lost in a garden if it's big enough and no one's around to remind her that there are other things to do.

She lives in New Hampshire, where the weather is beautiful and the autumn colors are amazing.

Manufactured by Amazon.ca
Bolton, ON